Praise for *Confederate Conspiracy*

In his compelling second book, D. Bruce Coryell brings back Irish immigrant Caleb Quinn and his ally Beau Carroll in a novel of treachery and violent revenge. A counterfeit conspiracy at the end of the American Civil War threatens the strength of the newly united nation. *Confederate Conspiracy* is a story of faith, doubt, and ultimate courage set in a time of divisive issues. Coryell writes as if he were there, evoking both the atmosphere of the wild frontier and the languid streets of New Orleans. The story is transporting and brilliantly alive with the mood of the day and with the action and adventure that is Coryell's style.

Ann Golias, author

The end of America's Civil War left the nation in a very fragile and precarious state. The victorious Federal government was bankrupt and the defeated South was utterly destroyed. Putting this nation back together was made even harder by a few die-hard Confederates who still wanted an independent Confederate nation.

Enter Captain Drummond, a Confederate officer who was brutally treated at Camp Douglas, a notorious federal prison in Chicago. Released from Camp Douglas, Captain Drummond became as brutal as his prison guards and devised a counterfeit scheme that would bankroll a new Confederate South and bankrupt the Federal North.

When some of these extraordinarily well printed counterfeit notes began to surface, President Johnson had to take quick and decisive action to maintain the federal monetary system. He called on Beau Carroll who in turn called on Caleb Quinn to help him find the counterfeiters and bring them to justice before a total monetary collapse.

As in his first book, *When the Night Bird Calls,* Caleb, Beau and their cohorts have plenty of villains to subdue and action is fast and furious on every page. Coryell weaves in real people, i.e. John Hill (a story of his own), real places and real events to make *Confederate Conspiracy* a must read if you like historical action novels.

Bruce Coryell is the new Louis L'Amour!

Tipton Golias
Chairman & Founder – Helena Laboratories,
ETOCO, L.P. and a history buff

Confederate Conspiracy
The Saga of Caleb Quinn

By D. Bruce Coryell

Published by D. Bruce Coryell
San Marcos, Texas

TO PURCHASE COPIES OF THE NOVEL WRITE OR
EMAIL:
D. BRUCE CORYELL
509 REIMER AVENUE
SAN MARCOS, TX 78666
dccoryell@yahoo.com

ROBIN,

I hope you
enjoy the book.

Bruce Coryell

A brief history of the characters included in the novel who were introduced in the author's first novel *When the Night Bird Calls*...

Beauregard Carroll – an immigrant from England who, through his resourcefulness and intelligence, made a name for himself in his new country. He was a friend of Joshua Webster, a printer from Belfast, a friendship that resulted in Beau becoming a mentor to young Caleb Quinn. Beau played a role as a counterspy for the Union during the Civil War.

Phillip Buckner – a freed slave and protégé of Beau Carroll, Phillip was owned by the Farrows of Washington, Louisiana until he was sold to Captain Varvil. Beau met Phillip while on the *Delta Queen*, Varvil's Mississippi river boat, and purchased his freedom from the Captain.

Caleb Quinn – an Irish immigrant and Civil War hero who came to the United States to escape pursuit from the British.

Christine Quinn – nee Pokusa, the wife of Caleb and a native of the state of Texas. She and her sister, along with another captive, Shannon Edwards, were rescued from the Comanche by Caleb, Tip Thomas, and Dos Baca.

Sean Michael Quinn – infant son of Caleb and Christine. He was named for his paternal grandfather and uncle who were murdered in Ireland before Caleb, then Liam O'Connell, left Ireland.

Matthew Moore – friend and neighbor of the Quinns, Matt and Caleb began their friendship on the *Osprey* during the long sea journey from Ireland to America.

Samantha Moore – wife of Matthew and a native of Scotland, she traveled to America with her husband to begin a life free of the tyranny of England.

Eryn Moore – the older daughter of Matthew and Samantha. She was conceived during the journey to America.

Emmilou Moore – the younger daughter of Matthew and Samantha.

Joshua Webster – boyhood friend of Liam O'Connell's father, Michael O'Connell, he aided Liam in his escape from the British by supplying him with falsified documents and his new identity as Caleb Quinn. Liam/Caleb was thus able to leave Ireland and aboard a ship bound for America.

Tip Thomas – Christine's brother-in-law and a Texas rancher, Tip formed a partnership with Caleb to rescue the Pokusa sisters from the Comanche.

Ann Thomas – nee Pokua, Christine's sister and the wife of Tip Thomas.

Gram Szeliga - the maternal grandmother of the Pokusa girls.

Shannon Edwards – the orphaned daughter of a Texas stage stop family who was captured by the same Comanche tribe that held Ann and Christine Pokusa. Shannon was rescued when Ann and Christine were.

Dos Baca – also known as Emilio Baca Jr., Dos is a lifelong friend of Tip, Ann and Christine. He was a member of the partnership that sought to rescue the sisters.

Rags Webber – the livery owner of the stables located in Liberty Hills, Texas.

Lucinda Baker – a long time friend of Beauregard Carroll, Phillip Buckner, and Caleb Quinn, who led a colorful life. Her life stretched the gamut from Savannah debutante to Mississippi River gambler and on to the *B and B* circus clairvoyant. The present novel finds her the head mistress of a prominent New Orleans Academy for Girls.

Jean Duvall – a long time friend of Beauregard Carroll, Phillip Buckner, Lucinda Baker, and Caleb Quinn who was the trick shot artist of the *B & B* circus and a former member of the French Foreign Legion.

Uriah Cordell – former mountain man and ringmaster of the *B & B* circus. Uriah took Caleb under his wing, at the behest of Beau Carroll, when he first landed in the United States.

Joe Pokusa – father of Ann and Christine, he was a sniper for the Confederate army and had a reputation as a sharpshooter that rivaled that of Caleb. He was killed by Caleb during one of the final battles of the Civil War.

Whitey Varvil – captain and owner of the *Delta Queen*, a floating gambling house riverboat that ran the Mississippi River from New Orleans through St. Louis and points north. He was an intimate of Lucinda Baker who frequently traveled/gambled on the *Delta Queen* in her youth.

National honor is national property of the highest value.

James Monroe
first inaugural address,
4 March 1817

Part 1

I think there is one higher office than president and I would call that patriot.

~Gary Hart

Chapter 1
The Conspiracy

It was shortly before midnight when Beauregard Carroll, escorted by the same presidential aide who had permitted his access earlier in the evening, left the White House. He traveled by way of the secret tunnel he had used during the Civil War when meeting with President Lincoln. Beau was one of only a few men who knew of the ten-foot-high and nine-foot-wide tunnel that had been built during the reconstruction of the White House after it was burned by the British in 1814. The British had narrowly missed capturing President Madison, his wife, Dolly, and his stepson, along with some of the country's most priceless documents, prompting the Army to be given the responsibility of devising a way to ensure the escape of future presidents should there be a threat on the White House similar to the one involving Madison. To the army fell the formidable task of building an escape tunnel in absolute secrecy while under the open gaze of the public. A public who would more than likely treat the entire construction project as a tourist attraction, making it all the more difficult to keep the tunnel a secret.

The army began by assembling a group of trusted engineers, many of whom would later be rumored to belong to the Order of Masons, and who, in turn, hired eighty non-English speaking miners from more than a dozen countries. These men were divided into two groups of forty with one group beginning their tunneling from below the basement of the White House kitchen and the second group starting their tunneling within a large military warehouse located more than a thousand yards to the south of the White House.

Neither group of miners knew where or when the other group began its tunneling, nor did they know the two tunnels were designed to converge in the middle. No explosives were used during the excavation, leaving the work to be done by men using only picks and shovels, a grueling job given the heat that collected underground. A few select miners and engineers completed the final twenty feet of digging which joined the two tunnels.

Upon completion of the project all the foreign miners, who had been told they were working on a new sewer system, were split up and assigned to army engineering projects hundreds of miles away and, whenever possible, isolated from one another. No record of the tunnel ever existed in any government or civilian agency records, leaving its presence to be passed down from president to president and the few men they trusted with the knowledge of its existence. Beauregard Carroll was one of those men.

Carrying a single oil-burning lamp as he sloshed through the shallow pools of water covering most of the tunnel floor, Beau was acutely aware that for reasons of security the tunnel, now more than fifty years old, had seldom been maintained during those years and with its moisture damaged shoring and leaking ceiling was subject to caving in at any moment. Despite this threat and the slight claustrophobic tendencies he was feeling, most of his thoughts revolved around replaying in his mind the conversation he'd had with the President.

****

"Mr. Carroll," said the President, "months prior to my taking over this office, President Lincoln confided in me about the service you rendered our country during the war. He also, in no uncertain terms, told me that you could be completely trusted and were the man he would call on if he needed the services of someone who would discretely take on the most difficult assignments. Now, with the latter in mind, I am asking you to once again come to your country's aid."

Despite previous meetings with President Lincoln, Beau was still somewhat in awe of the office; an awe which could be heard in the timbre of his voice as he softly replied, "You may ask anything of me, Sir."

"Mr. Carroll, I knew that would be your answer even before you sat down, but I must caution you, what I ask will be extremely dangerous for you and anyone working with you. This endeavor must also be treated with the utmost security. As such, only you and whomever you recruit to help you will know the exact nature of the mission I have set out for you."

"I understand, Sir, and my answer remains the same."

Before continuing, President Johnson took a long look at his guest. What he saw was a man slight of build, perhaps in his early forties, with a soft voice and deep-set intelligent eyes. In other words, not someone who looked like the dynamic hero of the Civil War he knew Beau to be, but more in appearance an average citizen, rather like a bookkeeper or personal assistant, someone seldom noticed in a crowd or even at a small gathering. President Johnson realized the man sitting across the desk from him was perfectly suited to be a spy, a man who could disappear at will.

"Except for his height he's very much like Abe," he thought, "a man of exceeding intelligence hidden behind an ordinary appearance."

Leaning forward and placing his elbows on the walnut desk top the President continued, "Here's the situation facing us. I have reliable information from agents in the field that there is a conspiracy a float to flood the entire country with counterfeit U.S. dollars. Two of our agents working in the South stumbled upon what was at first perceived to be minor cases of forgery emanating from New Orleans and Galveston, and involving our five and ten dollar greenbacks being distributed through local banks. Because the problem seemed localized to those cities neither report was given any real degree of attention by the Secret Service, but the agents were told to continue with their investigations. That was a month ago. Since then bogus money has started showing up as far away as New Mexico, Georgia and Maryland. You should also be aware we have been unable to make contact with either agent. Neither has been heard from since shortly after their reports were brought to the attention of me and their superiors."

Over the next hour, Beau, trying to memorize every word the President spoke, listened as the story fully unfolded.

The President finished with what amounted to a warning, "We must stop them at all costs. Failure to do so could bring about the fall of the federal government as we know it, and would open the distinct possibility of putting our western states and territories into the hands of a foreign power. If this were to happen it would be a never ending threat to our national security. Also, we must never forget this country you and I call home is a nation of immigrants, and God willing, will always be so. They have come to this country to build homes and a future and will need access to the lands in the west if they and this country are to reach their potential."

"I agree, Mr. President, but if I may be allowed to ask one question?"

"By all means," replied Johnson.

"Why," asked Beau, "have you given me, with my limited resources in terms of manpower, this mission which is so vital to our government? Why not the military or the Secret Service? For that matter, why not the Pinkerton Detective Agency?"

The President replied without any hesitation for they were courses of action he had considered when he was first made aware of the plot.

"I lack confidence in the army's ability, meaning that of my generals, to keep a secret, and should the seriousness of this conspiracy become public knowledge it could and most probably would cause a run on the banks. If a run should occur history may record that we, meaning this government and this presidency, were the instruments of our own demise... as for the Secret Service, they deal mostly with paperwork and are new to their duties. They lack the field experience needed for this job. Also, while they have been mildly effective at uncovering minor fraud and corruption in the northern states, they have little familiarity with the southern areas of this country. You, on the other hand, spent quite a bit of time working in the South during the war, and may still have valuable contacts there"

"And the Pinkertons?" asked Beau.

"I thought of them at first but decided against using them. As spies and security agents they did invaluable work during the war, but I have learned through politics not to overly trust men of ambition, and Allan Pinkerton is certainly a man of strong ambition. You, as opposed to Pinkerton, have a history of service which leads me to believe you have no personal agenda, and that your singular ambition is to serve and protect this country, even if it involves great risk to yourself."

Feeling slightly embarrassed by the President's compliment, Beau could not reply. However, it did occur to him that the President's words could also have described the man himself.

Beau had been studying the President's face during their long meeting and was dismayed by what he saw. The President looked bone-tired to the point of collapse. He sat round-shouldered, slightly slumped forward in his chair. His deep-set dark eyes were lined with fatigue. Beau knew some of the President's appearance could be attributed to the lateness of the hour but most of it, he speculated, was brought on by the constant series of attacks and opposition he endured from his political enemies. This good man, Beau knew, was being hit from all sides, by Northern and Southern sympathizers and politicians alike.

Congressmen and senators from the Union states wanted to make political gains by stopping him from carrying out Lincoln's plans for reconstruction, while the new representatives from the South despised the Tennessean as a traitor who had sided with the Union during the war. As such, they saw him as a man they did not want to cooperate with in any way, even if the lack of such needed cooperation was injurious to their beloved South. Johnson was a man caught between the proverbial "rock and a hard place" as he continuously battled with both sides of Congress over Reconstruction.

Notwithstanding the seriousness of the attacks against Johnson, Beau knew that words spoken recently by Senator Doolittle regarding the President were a true description of the man, "He is of bilious temperament, of strong intellect, indomitable energy, and iron will. I should say the strongest feature of all is that of stern justice, mingled with a genuine hatred of all forms of aristocracy and oppression, and patriotism so ardent that it amounts to a passion, almost a religion."

Beau's thoughts were suddenly interrupted when the President opened a desk drawer and removed an envelope with a very visible presidential seal imprinted on it.

"This," said Johnson as he handed the envelope across the desk to Beau, "identifies you as being a U.S. Marshall and gives you authority over any military or civilian authority whose services you deem necessary."

Beau took the envelope and tapped it lightly on his palm, "Thank you, Mr. President, but with your approval I could use two more such letters. One would be for a Phillip Buckner and the other for Caleb Quinn."

"Certainly," replied the President as he picked up a small hand bell and rang it.

The bell tinkled only a few times when one of the doors to the office was opened by the same aide Beau had met earlier, and who had undoubtedly been stationed just outside the office. Beau's appraisal of the man revealed he was as ordinary looking as any man he could imagine, even himself. He looked to be in his thirties and was dressed in a plain grey suit worn over a rumpled white shirt. Mutton chop sideburns and wire-rimmed glasses did nothing to take away from the plainness of his appearance.

"Yes, Sir?" asked the man in a small voice that sounded like that of a boy caught between puberty and early manhood.

"Mr. Chandler," said the President, "Mr. Carroll will need two more letters of Presidential Authority for…"

The President's words were left hanging as he looked from his aide to Beau.

"For Phillip Buckner, P-h-i-l-l-i-p B-u-c-k-n-e-r, and Caleb Quinn, C-a-l-e-b Q-u-i-n-n," said Beau.

"Very good, Sir," said the aide who immediately backed through the doorway and eased the door closed behind him.

"I'm not familiar with Phillip Buckner," the President told Beau as the door was being closed, "but the name Caleb Quinn seems to be one I've heard before."

"Caleb was one of Berdan's snipers and some of his exploits during the war were chronicled in several of the larger Eastern newspapers."

"And Buckner?" asked the President, more to kill time while the requested letters were being prepared than due to a lack of trust in Beau's judgment of his people.

"Phillip is a freed slave who has worked with me for many years. Both he and Caleb are well suited for the task ahead and can be trusted completely."

Several minutes of light conversation followed before a tapping on the door was heard and Mr. Chandler reentered the room. Moments later, after signing the letters, the President handed the two wax-sealed envelopes to his aide who passed them to Beau.

The aide, after asking, "Is there anything else, Mr. President?" was waved off and exited.

Immediately thereafter Beau left the President's office through the same door and was a bit surprised to see the President's aide standing only inches away and covering a yawn with the sleeve of his coat.

"I guess we could all use some sleep," he said to Chandler as they made their way toward the White House kitchen and the entry to the tunnel.

Entering the tunnel prompted Beau's thoughts to turn to his former President. He couldn't help thinking about the Lincoln assassination. He had never been able to shake from his mind the suspicion that the murder of his President and friend might have been the work of a far flung conspiracy possibly involving both foreign interests and vengeance-seeking Confederates other than John Wilkes Booth. Was Booth simply a pawn used by men in the shadows of government to further their own agendas? After his capture, why was Jefferson Davis spared the wrath of the northern public and never brought to trial to face charges of treason? Why was it never mentioned in northern newspapers that war materials made in the north were sold to Confederate states during the war? It was a mystery to him why these questions and many others remained unanswered.

Reaching the end of the tunnel and proceeding to the storehouse's vestibule Beau opened the door just enough to look out at the street, expecting to see a carriage waiting for him. There was none. No carriage, no people, only an empty street. Trying to ease his worry Beau's thoughts shifted to the President's departing words and the three envelopes he now carried.

Chapter 2
Lurking Danger

Phillip Buckner climbed over the final rung of the rusting fire escape leading to the roof of the four-story hotel. After pausing a full minute at the top to listen for any noise or voices that didn't belong there, he slid noiselessly over the raised brick ledge running the entire distance around the building's roof. Moving his head ever so slowly, he looked 180 degrees around, noting two structures near the center of the roof. The first was a round, three-foot high, raised platform holding a row of wooden chairs and an unlit lamp hanging from a post. The platform itself was undoubtedly used by the hotel's patrons to view the Washington DC landscape, by either day or night, and in any direction. The second structure enclosed the doorway which Phillip surmised led to the stairs which provided the same patrons access to the roof. He saw nothing that indicated any threat and for a moment thought his precaution had been for naught.

Just as he was about to make his way back down to the alley behind the hotel a light breeze carried the smell of smoke from a strong cigar to his wide nostrils. Someone was on the roof, probably concealed from view by the stairway enclosure. Phillip instantly switched his thinking from someone cautiously investigating a possible threat to that of a man ready to single-handedly eliminate an actual one.

After slowly raising his pants leg and removing a thin knife from his soft-soled high top boot he silently moved behind the enclosure peering around it toward the front of the hotel. At that exact moment a figure sitting next to the roof's edge nearest the street created a small shower of sparks by crushing out a cigar.

"Thank you for pointing the way," said Phillip to himself, still not certain the figure posed a real threat.

It was possible the man might simply be a solitary hotel patron enjoying a smoke as he took in the late night view of the city.

"But then," he told himself, "you would most likely be sitting in a chair on the platform, not hidden as you are behind the roof's balustrade."

His final doubts as to the figure's intentions disappeared when the man raised a scoped rifle, placed it on the ledge, and pointed it down toward the streets below and directly in line with where Beau would be making his exit from the warehouse onto the street.

Phillip, although aware of the deadliness of the situation, couldn't keep a small smile of satisfaction off his mahogany colored face. "For an assassin you sure are one stupid son-of-a-bitch when it comes to knowing how to stay undetected."

A minute later, the would-be assassin felt the point of a knife pressed against the back of his neck and a massive hand pushing his face into the roof's ledge.

"I suggest you first take your hand off the rifle and then we'll discuss why you're here," whispered a deep voice coming from only a foot behind him.

The man responded in a way that almost caught Phillip unprepared, but Phillip knew better than to underestimate any opponent, even one in a seemingly helpless position. The assassin released the rifle, but then immediately tried to throw a right elbow behind his head in an attempt to dislodge the knife at his neck, or at the least

11

strike his attacker in the face. It was a fatal lack of judgment on the part of the would-be killer who barely felt the knife as it slipped into his neck and severed the carotid artery causing the man's eyes to fully open in surprise as his body jerked twice and then lay still. No surgeon with a scalpel could have brought a more precise or silent ending to a man's life.

"You," said Phillip as he cleaned off the knife on the dead man's coat collar, "needed less courage and a lot more common sense."

A half hour later, the carriage driven by Phillip rounded a corner and slowly approached the warehouse.

Chapter 3
Courtesy of Pigeons

Beau had been waiting anxiously just inside the warehouse vestibule. Their pre-arranged plan was for Phillip to pass by the warehouse at half-hour intervals until Beau appeared. Almost twice that time had passed before he spotted Phillip and the carriage rounding the corner.

Such a break in planning was out of character for Phillip and something causing Beau concern. Leaving the vestibule and stepping onto the sidewalk, he glanced to the left and then to the right, looking for anyone hiding in the shadows. Seeing nothing out of the ordinary, he moved quickly to the carriage's door and was mildly surprised when Phillip patted the seat next to him, indicating he should sit up front instead of his customary place inside the carriage. It did not go unnoticed by Beau that this was a second odd bit of behavior on Phillip's part.

Without hesitation Beau grasped a handhold and swung nimbly up onto the seat.

"Trouble?" asked Beau.

"You could call it that. We've been compromised," said Phillip as he got the bay gelding moving with a light flick of the reins.

With his other hand he passed Beau a rumpled yellow envelope. Opening the unsealed packet Beau removed a quarter-inch thick stack of very crisp five and ten dollar bills. Intrigued by the money, especially after his recent conversation with the President about counterfeiting, Beau reached over and placed a hand on the reins.

"Please pull over under the nearest lighted lamp so that I can get a better look at this money," he directed Phillip.

After the carriage came to a stop at a corner only a block away, Beau carefully examined the top three five dollar bills. The serial numbers were identical.

"You got these courtesy of....?"

"Pigeons," replied a stone-faced Phillip.

Beau let a few moments pass allowing Phillip's statement to sink in.

"You did say pigeons?" questioned Beau.

"Yes Sir," said Phillip, enjoying the puzzled look on his friend's face, a look he had hoped to see. "It was pigeons that let me know someone might be on the Hotel Monaco's roof."

"After I dropped you off, I parked the carriage between two buildings on F Street so I wouldn't draw anyone's attention to it or you. It was about an hour ago when I noticed a flock of pigeons suddenly fly off the roof. I'm not an expert on birds but any city kid knows pigeons don't ordinarily take to the air at night unless, of course, they're disturbed or threatened. In this case I didn't see any owls or hawks lurking about."

Beau sat silently and stoically, waiting patiently for Phillip's story to further unfold.

"So, being the curious fellow I am, I circled back behind the hotel and used the fire escape to get to the roof. That's where I found a shooter with a scoped rifle beading

14

in on 15th Street, exactly where you would have come out of the warehouse. I have little doubt he planned to take his shot the second you stepped onto the sidewalk. I had intended to strike up a brief conversation with the gentleman, but when he resisted I did what I had to do."

Beau knew Phillip was a natural hunter and unsurpassed at silently stalking prey whether it was man or beast. Knowing what would have surely transpired, he asked, "And the body?"

"I deposited it in the alley after removing the man's shoes and turning out his pockets. Anybody doing an investigation will figure it was a simple mugging that turned ugly."

"And the rifle?"

"You've almost got your feet on it," replied Phillip. "I kept it thinking it might come in handy in case the deceased had friends."

"Was there any way of telling who he was?"

"As I said, he gave me no chance to exchange pleasantries with him before his untimely demise, but by his actions I believe he had a military background. Most civilians would have submitted to being caught considering the knife I had at the back of his neck, but he thought enough of his fighting ability to resist. It was a fatal mistake on his part."

"Were there any identification papers on him?"

"No, the only thing he had on him was the money and it doesn't say much"

"It says more than you might think," replied Beau. "If we could trace it back to its origin it might be able to point me toward who wants me dead, and who among the President's staff compromised us, although I believe I may already know whom the person in question is."

After a pause to think, Beau continued his questioning of the events looking for further information of any kind.

"I'm sure there was a gun case."

"Also at your feet, but I looked and there's nothing there. It's a standard issue a thousand people could own, and has nothing on it to indicate ownership. The shooter could have bought the rifle or the gun case at any gun shop. It's also possible he could have picked them up during the war or afterwards from a returning soldier."

Beau had a suspicion there was more, that, as was Phillip's usual way of telling a story, he was saving the best for last.

"So, my friend, was there anything else of interest? Something you may be saving to impress me?"

"Well," said Phillip, slightly irritated that Beau could read him so easily, "there were the two tattoos. One was a fleur-de-lis on the inside of his right forearm."

"And the other, if you don't mind?"

"Much more elaborate," said Phillip, "it was on his left arm and showed a sailing ship. It's hard to say exactly what kind of sailing ship because both tattoos were blurry and looked like the work of an amateur."

"That's interesting," remarked Beau, feigning just a touch of sarcasm, "but need I remind you it's not uncommon for sailors to have tattoos of ships, and if the person was French, to also have a fleur-de-lis?"

"True, true," said Phillip, "but this ship had a name written above the tattoo. It was the *Sea Lady.*"

"You're positive it said '*Sea Lady*'?" asked Beau. "You're absolutely certain?"

Phillip realized the ship's name meant something to his friend and mentor.

"I'm positive it was *Sea Lady.* Does that name have some significance?"

The question brought back a troublesome memory for Beau.

"It does," answered Beau. "As you know, during the war I played a role in our navy's interception of Confederate blockade runners. The *Sea Lady* was one of only a few blockade runners that when intercepted with no chance of getting away, chose to fight rather than surrender. As a consequence, a year before the end of the war she he was sunk by Union gunboats with all but a few of her crew lost. Her sinking was a direct result of my giving her course and arrival time to the Union navy. It wasn't an end result I favored because good men, some I knew first hand, went down with her. Sadly, that is often the painful price of war."

Phillip listened, aware that Beau, unlike himself, could deeply regret the loss of a man's life, even if that life belonged to an enemy.

After several seconds of reflection, Beau began to summarize the information.

"So, what we have is possibly a Frenchmen, or perhaps an Acadian, paid with counterfeit money to kill me. It also stands to reason he was a crew member of the *Sea Lady,* and may have been on her when she went down. I might add the *Sea Lady*'s home port was New Orleans."

"There is one other thing," said Phillip.

"And what would that be?"

"Our sailor friend truly liked a good cigar."

****

An hour later the carriage pulled to a stop in front of the Dumbarton Street residence Beau used as his District of Columbia home.

"We need to leave in the morning, no later than ten o'clock," he told Phillip, "and you'll need to pack for an extended trip, some of it in cold country."

Beau quickly entered the house and went directly to the basement where he spent the next hour tapping out messages on his personal telegraph. Thanks to President Lincoln's benevolence and equal appreciation for secrecy, the telegraph was the only one held by a private citizen in the District of Columbia, or for that matter, any other city within the United States. Beau knew a telegram was only as private as the telegraph operator on the other end made it, and for that reason the messages he sent were as vague as possible.

He also wrote two letters, one to the President and another to someone who had served as President Lincoln's personal aide on the household staff; a black man whom Beau trusted explicitly to deliver the letter personally to President Johnson. Both letters were placed in a single envelope. With this done and knowing he needed sleep, he went back upstairs. Lying down on a settee in the drawing room he closed his eyes.

Four hours later his internal clock told him it was time to get up and make the final preparations for the trip. After packing a single leather travel bag with clothes, cash, weapons, and several different sets of identification papers, he moved to the front entrance vestibule where he spent several minutes peering through the specially made one-way glass, searching the street in front of the house for any sign of a threat or anything out of the ordinary. It was an exercise in caution that had served him well for many years, and was now even more necessary because as Phillip stated, "We've been compromised."

Seeing the approach of the carriage, Beau took one more look about and then left the house. The carriage, driven by a man Beau had hired on several other occasions, had hardly pulled to a stop as Beau threw his bag inside and took a seat across from Phillip.

"And just where is it we're going?" Phillip asked even before his friend was fully seated.

"Our first stop is the residence of a friend I met during the war, and the second stop will be the train station," answered Beau.

As Beau settled into his seat he noticed the gleaming handle of a good-sized revolver sticking out of his companion's waist band. He knew the revolver was only

19

one of several weapons, some concealed and some not, that Phillip carried at times of real or potential danger. He, himself, never went out without at least one sleeve gun and often two.

"And we are catching the train to…?" asked Phillip.

Casually leaning back in the seat, Beau crossed his legs and removed two cigars from the inside pocket of his coat. Handing one to Phillip, he struck a match which both men used to light their cigars. Then releasing a generous puff of smoke he replied, "According to my sources, the mountains of northern Georgia are a beauty to behold this time of year."

Chapter 4
Renegade Cherokee

It was a cold morning in late October when Caleb Quinn and Matthew Moore left the isolated mountain town of Robbinsville, North Carolina, and headed southwest back to their homes just across the state line in Georgia. Four brood mares, all proven and all roped together, trailed behind them along with a paint pony Matt had bought for his older daughter, Eryn. They had made good buys, taking advantage of the owners wanting to sell their stock before they were forced to either grain or hay feed the animals through the cold and grassless winter.

"Been a while since we've had Indian trouble," said Matt.

"I'll take your word for it," replied Caleb, recalling the warning given to them by the last of the horse sellers back in Robbinsville.

"If you're goin' back along the Nantahala River keep a sharp eye out for Indians," the man had warned. "Seems a renegade Cherokee, called Bloody Bill, is leading raids on whites livin' around Bryson City and all the way down through the Nantahala Gorge."

Even though Caleb knew the way home would take them through the upper region of the Nantahala River area, he was not overly concerned. He and Matt had both fought in the war and had known their share of killing, of hard fighting, and both were armed with brand new Henry repeating rifles.

In fact, Matt was a one man mobile arsenal on horseback. Carried at various places on his body and saddle were the Henry, a short-barreled Remington shotgun, a hard hitting Schofield revolver, and a "Baja" Bowie-style knife with an eleven inch blade. Stuck in his waistband was a long-handled hand axe which Matt could throw accurately at a target over thirty-five feet away.

In addition to his Henry, Caleb was armed with a holstered 1860 model Colt revolver and, as always, his father's knife, the same knife he had carried since leaving Ireland as a sixteen-year-old fugitive running from the British.

They had been following the twisting mountain road for almost two hours when Caleb, riding in front, brought his Texas-bred buckskin to a halt. Slowly swinging out of the saddle he pretended to adjust his saddle straps.

"Make sure the lead lines to the mares are tied tight to the pommel," he whispered to Matt, "because unless I miss my guess we've got bad company up ahead, and you may need both hands to do some shooting."

"You spot some trouble?" asked a puzzled Matt.

On the trip into Robbinsville, using the same road they were now traversing, Caleb's military training had kicked in as he noticed a slight bend in the road, a bend that was now only a hundred yards or so ahead of them. When he first saw the bend in the road it occurred to him that if he were picking a spot for an ambush this would be it. Not only were the trees thick where they reached the road, but dozens of various sized boulders were scattered among them, offering solid cover and concealment to anyone setting up an ambush.

"I'm not positive," he told Matt, "but the hair on my arms is tingling and my buckskin just threw off two shivers and I don't think it's because of the cold."

"Ya think you and the buckskin can tell me how many there are?" asked Matt as he tightened up the lead lines.

"Matt, the horse probably knows but I'm not even sure they're there. However, I do know a fast way to find out."

Caleb jerked the Henry out of its saddle boot, took aim, and fired two shots, kicking up dirt to either side of a large boulder a few feet from the road. The echo from the shots was still resounding between the mountains when a group of as many as eight armed Indians burst from their hiding places in the trees, firing what had to be smoothed barreled muskets as they moved toward Caleb and Matt.

Their ambush had been detected too early to be immediately effective but the Indians still moved forward, confident of the advantage of their numbers and sure the two white men, like so many other white men before them, when faced by vastly superior numbers, would turn loose their string of horses and run. The Indians' opinion of the two white men they now faced was about to undergo a dramatic change.

The Indians were caught totally off-guard as Caleb and Matt, ignoring the bullets whizzing by them, emptied their Henry rifles into the advancing group of men, knocking down two of the three nearest the road and bringing an abrupt end to the charge by the others who were now desperately scrambling back into the cover of the trees.

After firing the last round in the Henry, Caleb shoved it back in the saddle boot, and with a "Come on" to Matt swung back into the saddle, drew his Colt and headed in the direction of the retreating Indians.

Matt put his empty rifle back in its boot, grabbed his shotgun out of the leather loop he used to attach it to the saddle and bellowed, "Right behind you."

He then kicked his horse in the ribs and let out a Rebel yell that could have been heard for miles around.

When Caleb was within revolver shot of the Indians he fired three shots that were instantly followed by two blasts from Matt's shotgun. There was no answering fire from the Indians who, expecting an easy ambush and not a full fledged attack from two crazy white men armed with rifles that fired an endless number of bullets, were now concerned only with the need to stay alive. The Indians scrambled up the steep slope of the hill, hoping the men on horseback would be unable to follow them into the rough, rock and tree-filled terrain. Two of the Indians left behind looked to be seriously wounded and it appeared a third would never raid again.

Matt and Caleb brought their horses to a stop where the Indians had vanished into the woods. Neither of them spoke while they scanned the nearest trees for any signs of the scattered Indians.

Reloading his shotgun, Matt asked, "You thinking about chasing after them?"

"Not in the least," came the reply as Caleb put six fresh shells in the Colt. "But you're certainly welcome to chase after them if you want to. Me, I'm getting gone from here as fast as this horse I'm sitting on will take me."

Matt knew Caleb wasn't entirely joking. Like Caleb, he had enough fighting experience to know you don't chase armed Indians into thick hilly woods if you want to live to see the next day. This was especially true when there were more of them than there were of you.

"Maybe I'll come back after them when next summer rolls around," Matt replied as he turned his horse back down the road. "Right now I just want to get us and these horses out of here while there ain't no new holes in me."

Minutes later the two men were heading home just as a soft snow, the first of the winter, began to fall.

****

Ten days had passed since Caleb's and Matt's return from their horse buying trip to western North Carolina. Neither man had mentioned the run-in they had with the renegade Indians to their wives, figuring it far wiser to protect them from the knowledge of future threats, but even more importantly to the two men, not giving Christine and Samantha a good excuse to say "No" to the plans the two men had of going hunting during the next few months.

By mutual agreement the two friends decided that unless they wanted to spend most of the winter stuck in their homes, their continued silence concerning their run in with the renegade Indians would be of paramount importance.

****

During the summer, and even more so during the past few weeks of fall, the Quinn and Moore families had been working, as Matt put it "from can see to can't see," preparing for the coming cold months. Acres of hay were cut and piled in their barns as high as the rafters. Barrels of grain for the horses, milk cows, cattle, and mules were stacked under the overhangs coming off the barns. Head high cords of firewood covered half their front porches while other stacks of cut logs and kindling were neatly piled between some of the larger trees growing close to their houses. Sausages, bacon, hams, geese, and turkey hung by the dozens in their smoke houses. Their root cellars were stuffed with bags and baskets of corn, potatoes, onions, beans, nuts, and cheeses. Jars of honey, vegetables and dried fruits, along with barrels of flour ground at the grist mill in Copper Hill filled their pantries. The two families were more than ready for whatever the winter threw at them.

Earlier that month Christine and Samantha had spent a day in Mineral Bluff buying books, sugar, coffee, spices, and woolen and cotton material to make shirts, pants, skirts, dresses; enough to keep them busy when the cold air seeping over the surrounding mountains forced them to spend much of their time inside. When they got back to the house the last thing they unloaded from the overburdened wagon was a new churn for making ice cream using a combination of cream, sugar, and vanilla syrup that would be mixed in the churn with a bucket full of clean snow. The Quinns and the Moores now had enough food and other provisions put back to last them through even the longest and harshest of winters their north Georgia mountains could throw at them.

To Caleb and Matt, now was the ideal time for them to resume their favorite preparation for the winter...hunting for bear. To wait any longer would mean the bears would have denned up for the winter and would be impossible to find under the usual blanket of heavy mountain snow.

Chapter 5
The Hunt

    Shortly after sunrise the old she bear led her one remaining cub up the mountain overlooking the Hiawassee River. She was wise in the ways of the two-legged creatures hunting them and wanted only to get as far away from them as possible.

    Three seasons earlier she had escaped almost certain death by climbing high into the branches of a tall ash tree and remaining there for a terrifyingly full afternoon and half the night as the fight between the groups of man things raged below her. When the gunfire had ceased and the men had been gone for more than an hour she finally felt it safe to descend from her tree top sanctuary. Even before her feet touched the ground her nostrils were assaulted by the smell of dead man-things and expended gunpowder. It was a frightening memory that caused her to spend the following three years away from man and in the most remote parts of Georgia's northern mountains.

    This knowledge of man-things and the death they brought also added to her desperate need to get away from the men now pursuing her and the male cub, the only cub left from a litter of three. It was this same male cub that was slowing their escape. The hungry cub, having been raised without ever encountering a human and now almost a year old, did not comprehend the danger man presented. The cub, despite his mother's grunts of disapproval, insisted on stopping several times to eat the last of the blackberries clinging to the bushes on either side of the narrow deer trail they were following up the mountain. Mother and cub instinctively knew the need to eat all they could, to put on as much fat as possible before they were forced into the long sleep. Neither of them could know it was this same fat that was largely responsible for their being hunted.

Caleb and Matt had been following the bear tracks since noon, hoping to make a kill but in no real hurry to do so. For them this hunt was more about the chase, about being in the outdoors, about the age old excitement of pursuing prey. They also knew that because neither man chose to raise pigs with all their accompanying bad smells, the pounds of rich bear fat and juicy meat would be a welcome addition to their tables. Venison, easy to come by due to the deer's liking for corn left over after the harvest, was tasty and made for a good meal, but with so little fat in it, a family could damn near starve to death no matter how much of it they ate. Fat-covered, belly-filling bear steaks were the real prize the two hunters sought for their families.

"Ain't no need to hurry," said Matt to his younger friend and neighbor as they stopped to drink from a small stream of water flowing out of a crevice between a large pile of rocks. "I wouldn't want you to wear out those weak young legs of yours."

"Yeah," replied Caleb, "and by the way you're huffing and puffing I worry about the prospect of you passing out and me having to haul your overweight old carcass back down this mountain."

"Don't go worrying too much on my account." came back Matt's lively retort. "If I get too wore out I'll just roll on down the way we come up and leave you lost and stranded."

Any further conversation temporarily ended as Matt took a seat on a flat rock and proceeded to stuff his cheek with a bulging wad of shredded tobacco. In response Caleb found a rock of his own, pulled out a corn cob pipe made by his own hand and already stuffed with tobacco, lit it, and settled back for a relaxing smoke.

Never one to miss a chance to throw a verbal barb at his young friend, Matt gave Caleb a look of disdain, "You might want to snuff out that smelly pipe unless you're trying to let every critter in these parts know we're here."

"Well, do me a favor," replied Caleb sending back his own verbal barb, "when we do get back to the chase let me lead so I don't risk slipping on the nasty spit you seem hell bent on covering everything with, including your chin."

With a short laugh and a spit of tobacco Matt wiped a bit of the drool off his chin, rose to his feet, and headed up the mountain at a fast pace, more rapid than before and far faster than necessary. Caleb smiled. He knew Matt was once again offering one of his beloved challenges of strength and stamina. Caleb would readily concede the contests of strength, but challenges of stamina were quite another thing. The fun-loving giant had been issuing these friendly fun challenges since the day he and Caleb first met years ago when both of them sailed on the same ship taking immigrants from Ireland to America.

"You're still stronger than me for sure," he hollered at Matt's back, "but I'll run your butt into the ground if that's what it takes to keep from hearing another one of your big brags or the sound of your incessant cackling."

Matt's mouth was too full of tobacco juice and laughter to offer any words in response.

For the next hour they continued tracking the bears but even in the inch deep snow somehow managed to lose the tracks when their quarry, out of luck or from some innate knowledge Matt and Caleb didn't think the she bear was capable of, turned off the deer trail. The bear walked through a stream for a distance of over a hundred yards, and then left the water by climbing out over flat rocks, finally returning to the trees all without leaving any discernable prints. It was Caleb, using some of the skills of sight and smell he had acquired as a young poacher in Ireland, who eventually found where the bears had left the rocks and moved back into the trees.

"Caleb," said Matt, "if I didn't know luck when I see it, I'd swear that long Irish nose of yours could smell a snake farting underwater."

Before Caleb could think of a suitable retort to toss back both men came to an abrupt stop. At their feet they could see more tracks, but tracks of men, not bear. They both knelt down and studied the indentations in the soft earth.

"It would appear to me," whispered Matt, "we ain't the only ones hunting bear."

Caleb heard Matt's words but did not reply until he had further studied the signs.

"I count three adults and one child or woman. You can see where the lacings of their moccasins left marks in the mud. You can also see the slight imprints of their toes which means the moccasins are well-worn."

"You sure?" asked Matt, "'cause most likely if they're moccasin tracks we're talking Indians."

"I'm sure," answered Caleb, "which leaves us with a decision to make. We can either be the smart men we think we are, and return empty-handed to our loving wives, or we can be stupid and stay on the hunt."

Matt, always more than willing to accept any challenge, large or small, gave Caleb the predictable answer,

"Seeing as how we've already wore out these bar by chasing them up the mountain, I figure they're ours until it gets decided differently."

The decision made, the two hunters moved out under a graying sky now releasing a storm of even heavier flakes of snow.

****

The first of the bears to die was the cub, struck through the chest and into the heart by a single arrow, and dead seconds after hitting the ground. The she bear was less fortunate. Having taken two musket balls, one to a lung and another which shattered her lower jaw, she was severely wounded and in a panic to escape her pain and her pursuers. The direction she chose to run was the easiest of ways, right back down the mountain and slightly away from but parallel to the path she had come up, and almost right at Caleb and Matt.

The shots fired into the she bear brought Caleb and Matt to a sudden halt as they tried to determine the exact direction and distance from which the shots had come. This was not a simple thing to do amidst these echoing mountains and the falling snow. They had been standing motionless and silent for a minute when they heard something or someone noisily crashing through the trees and brush and coming fast in their direction. Without words, using only hand signals and eyes to communicate, each man moved off the deer trail, Caleb to the left and Matt to the right, melting into the woods as they looked for whatever cover they could find among the nearly leafless brush, slender pine trees, and short evergreens.

The wounded bear, howling loudly in pain, came hurtling down the hill at full speed, concerned only with the need to escape the man things and oblivious to anything in front of her. It was Matt who took the shot.

The bullet from the Henry entered just above the right eye and exited out the back of her skull. She was dead even before she slid face down into the mixture of mud, leaves and snow, her agony ending only a few yards from Matt's place of concealment.

When Matt fired Caleb had been on one knee, breathing lightly, his body relaxed, his rifle cocked and pointing uphill in the direction of the oncoming noise. At the sound of the shot he made no move toward the dead bear but remained absolutely silent and motionless, listening and looking for the Indians who would most certainly be in hot pursuit of the wounded bear.

He saw nothing and heard nothing through the falling snow but the strange silence that always seems to follow a shot from a high-powered rifle. Taking a chance the Indians would still be well back from his position he moved ten more paces away from the trail and about twenty more paces uphill before lowering his body and pushing his way under the ground level branches of a small, snow covered evergreen. It was the only bit of cover he could find that would break up his silhouette while still affording him an open view up the mountain. He could no longer see or hear Matt but assumed he had either remained where he was or moved only a slight distance away to better cover.

Time passed. The snowfall, accompanied by a slight breeze, came down even harder and faster, making it difficult to perceive anything more than thirty feet away but not so difficult as to prevent Caleb from seeing three shadowy figures slowly emerge from the swirling curtain of snow.

The Indians were crouched low and moving cautiously but never all three of them at the same time. One or two would move, one or two would stay still, looking and listening, searching for the presence of whomever it was that fired the shot, ready to seek cover at a split second's notice, or if it became necessary, to fight. It was a tactic an admiring Caleb would have used in similar circumstances.

"It's a good way for men to stay alive when there are armed and possibly dangerous people about, but not in sight," he thought.

Caleb saw that two of the Indians carried ancient looking smooth bore muzzle-loading muskets which he doubted they'd had time to reload since firing at the bear. The third Indian carried a bow with an arrow at the ready and several more arrows in a quiver slung over his back. To Caleb's thinking it was the bowman who posed the greatest threat, and whom he would take out first if it came to a fight. The Indian who had left the smallest of the four tracks was not in sight.

Matt found himself directly in line with the approaching Indians with the dead bear separating them by less than thirty yards, a situation which neither concerned nor comforted him. To his stoic mind it was merely the way it was, nothing more than a problem to resolve. He watched calmly as the three Indians, spotting the dead bear, stopped as if one and scanned the area, seeking even the smallest sign of danger. Seeing none, yet knowing danger was there but likely hidden by the falling snow, they too sought concealment in the pines and evergreens.

For the next quarter hour all of the hunters held their positions, none of them willing to be the first to move and in the doing, perhaps be the first to either die or be wounded. They were all familiar with the rules of both hunting and war, and needed no one to tell them how easily even the slightest movement could be detected by an alert man or animal. For many men and animals, the first movement they made was often their last.

Chapter 6
The Proposition

It was Matt who finally broke the impasse.

"Are my Cherokee friends here to share with me the meat from the great gv-ni-ge-yo-na?" he shouted across the short distance separating him and the Indians.

At the sound of Matt's voice the Indians were mildly surprised but neither moved nor immediately responded. To their trained ears what they heard was the voice of a man who seemed to be of good size but yet was able to easily hide as a smaller man might. What did really surprise them was that the man knew enough of the "civilized Cherokee tongue" to correctly use the word for black bear.

Caleb saw the two Indians carrying the muskets look at the bow hunter asking with their eyes how they should respond to the voice. He now knew with a certainty the bow hunter was the leader.

"We hear you and are pleased you so generously offer to share our kill with us," replied the bow hunter in perfect English. "I am A-i-sv E-lo-we-hi, called Walks Silent in your English, and I offer to share with you what E-Du-Da, the great giver of all things, has bestowed on us."

Walks Silent's words, spoken as they were with a degree of humor, only confirmed what Matt's eyes had already told him. These Indians, like Caleb and himself, were hunters, not renegades, and posed little threat unless threatened.

"I am Matthew Moore, and we accept your offer."

He then rose from his hiding place, shook the snow from his shoulders, and stepped into view of the Indians with his rifle held in two hands and pointed at the sky.

Walks Silent also stepped forward until the two men stood face-to-face on either side of the dead bear.

"You spoke the word we," said Walks Silent as he shot a quick look past Matt. "Are there other hunters with you?"

"Just one, me, Caleb Quinn," came a voice from behind the three Indians.

The Indians, caught totally off-guard, snapped their heads around as if they had been slapped. What they saw was a white man, rifle held in the crook of his arms, standing only a few yards away and smiling at them.

The sudden appearance of the tall white man was unsettling to them. Raised in the outdoors since birth they were totally unaccustomed to having anything, man or animal, approach them so closely without being detected. To the superstitious Indians it was as if a ghost had materialized out of air and snow.

Caleb could see a moment of fear in the eyes of the bow hunter's companions. It was an understandable fear, Caleb thought, knowing of the many times the Cherokee had been mistreated and lied to by white men and other Indians alike.

In response he slowly placed the butt of his rifle on the ground, showing the Indians he meant them no harm and was not afraid to stand before them in a nearly defenseless position. The two musket-carrying Indians quickly matched

Caleb's example, thereby breaking any tension between the two groups of men.

Within minutes the men had agreed that each of them would get an equal share of the bear's fat and meat. The boy who had been left behind with the bear cub would have it as his share. Removing their knives from their scabbards, Caleb, Matt and Walks Silent began the arduous task of skinning out the bear while the other Indians headed back up the mountain to help the boy dress out the cub.

After completing the job of dressing out the bear, the men wrapped most of the cut up pieces of meat and fat in bear skin but left out enough juicy meat from the rump of the she bear to make a sizable meal for all the hunters.

With gunpowder and flint the Indians started a fire and the meat was soon being slow roasted on yet green pine branches held over the flames. After only a few minutes of holding the meat over the fire the Indians removed handfuls of the still bloody meat and began stuffing it into their mouths as fast as they could swallow it.

As they ate, Caleb and Matt watched the Indians and became increasingly concerned by what they saw. All of the Indians spoke English and wore, except for their deer-skin moccasins, white man's clothes. But their clothes were torn and thread-bare, and too thin to keep anyone warm in the chilly mountain air. Even more discomforting was the manner in which they ate. They had been in a frenzy to down the half-cooked bear meat; even to the point of burning their fingers as they wolfed it down. They swallowed large mouthfuls seemingly without first chewing it or taking the time to savor it. Matt and Caleb could only watch in silence as within minutes every morsel of the meat, every bit of the fat, had disappeared.

Caleb could see that the Indians, especially the boy, looked gaunt and emaciated, with sunken eyes and cheeks and frail bodies. They were thin to the point they could barely move without a determined effort. It was the same tired look of starvation Caleb had seen much of during his boyhood in Ireland, and recognized as a look too often followed by death. It was a look he hated to the core of his being.

What Caleb also noticed was the Cherokee were different in appearance than the Indians he had encountered during the war or in Texas. Those Indians had been rather short and stocky with round-shaped faces and wide blunt noses. The Cherokee gathered around the fire were tall with square faces, straight well-shaped noses, and seemed almost European in appearance. Their reddish colored skin did nothing to detract from their handsome features and look of intelligence.

With their meal finished Caleb lit his pipe from a flaming twig, took several puffs to ensure it stayed lit, and then offered it to Walks Silent.

Walks Silent refused the pipe with a backhand wave of his hand and a soft spoken, "Thank you, my friend," as he removed from his pant's pocket a fine looking ornately carved pipe, "I have my own pipe but I could use some tobacco if you have it to spare."

Removing his tobacco pouch from his pocket, Caleb leaned forward across the waning fire and handed it to Walks Silent. Both men then sat back to enjoy their pipe smoking.

After several minutes of contemplating the crackling fire, Caleb was the first to speak.

"Matt and I are a long walk from our homes and have decided we would rather not bear the burden of carrying so much meat so far. We ask our new friends to keep our share except for the front claws. I wish to make them into a necklace for my son."

It was a request Caleb made, not to acquire the claws but to balance out the giving of their share of the meat and fat to the Indians. In doing so he hoped to avoid infringing on the pride of his new friends.

Walks Silent pondered the offer for a moment, fully understanding that the easy to like white man had skillfully designed his words to protect the Cherokee's pride while with the same words offering them food it was obvious they desperately needed. It was an unlikely act of compassion he was surprised to find coming from a white man, but already he was coming to realize these white men were out of the ordinary and might be trusted.

"I happily accept your kind offer," replied Walks Silent. "My people below have need of the meat for we have long been without a good kill. I regret that we have no way to repay you except with our friendship."

"We would want nothing more than to be your friends," said Caleb, "but now I would ask this. Where is your home and family?"

It was a question to which he thought he knew the answer, an answer which would set into action a plan he devised while watching the Indians eat. He had not discussed the plan with Matt, but had little doubt his friend would favor it.

"Our home is still in the making," replied Walks Silent as he stared into the fire, "but for now we are camped east of here along the Valley River."

"And before that?"

"You have heard of nu-na-hi-du-na-tlo-hi-lu-i, the trail of those who cried?" asked Walks Silent, who had recognized Caleb's Irish accent as foreign and thought he might still be too new to this country to be aware of its history. In that he was wrong.

Caleb was well aware of the tragic 1838 movement of the Cherokee people to the Oklahoma territory. It was a journey forced on them by the federal government so that the rich Cherokee lands could be taken legally by whites. It was a tragedy and a crime which cost the Cherokee not only the lands they had lived on for hundreds of years but also thousands of lives and unspeakable misery. It was an act of prejudice and greed that Caleb knew was not unlike that which the English had imposed on the Irish of his homeland.

"Yes," replied Caleb, "I've heard of it. I have heard the white man call it the Trail of Tears."

After fully drawing smoke from the pipe into his lungs, Walks Silent then blew out the smoke and continued his story, "My family was rounded up and forced out of their village at Fightingtown Creek, near what the white man now calls Ducktown. The soldiers came to the village from the place along the Hiawassee River called Tianusi-yi, the Leech place, which whites know as Murphy. They had with them hundreds of my people who were rounded up from our mountain homes to the east and kept at Fort Butler until the government decided it was time to move us out west to Indian Territory. Even though our village was home

40

to more than one hundred of our people, we were allowed to take with us only what little food and clothing we could carry in our hands and on our backs."

"I was born on the trail of those who cried," said Walks Silent as he continued to look into the fire.

"I was one of the few newborns to survive. My brother and sister, a brother and sister I never knew, did not survive the walk even through they were older than I. Their bones and those of many of my relatives lie buried in western Arkansas somewhere along the Illinois River."

After taking another deep puff from his pipe Walks Silent continued, "We were marched over eight hundred miles to our new "home" in the Indian Territory, a dry hot place of big winds also called Oklahoma. During the almost thirty years I lived there my people never stopped talking about our real home in these incredible mountains where we now stand. Through stories they told of its beauty, the many flowing rivers that stayed full year round, the abundance of game, the fertile earth that gave a bountiful harvest even without watering. For me and my people it was a dream land, one so vastly different from the poor land we were forced to live on."

"But you are here now."

"Yes. Six months ago I led the men you see here, and the women and girl left back at our camp, out of Oklahoma. We left at night with our wagons, our horses and mules, our tools, everything we needed to build a new life in these mountains. At first, by traveling over the more unused roads we had little trouble, but when we reached the Tennessee River above Chattanooga white men, some wearing hoods, took almost all we had, leaving us only the clothes on our backs, my bow, and the two muskets the

41

women had managed to hide in their clothing. Despite the loss of almost everything we had, we pushed on, determined to return to our mountains or die. I sometimes thought it was as if my people were once again on the trail of those who cried but this time traveling in the opposite direction."

"What will you do now?" asked Caleb, as he once again thought of his plan to aid these Cherokee he had already come to admire.

"Find our own land, try to live free," came the reply, "in the Cherokee way but also in the way of the whites. To become as your people think of it, 'civilized Indians.' It is the only way for us to survive, to see our children and their children live in this land."

"Walks Silent," said Caleb, "I have a proposition to make you and your people, a proposition which will benefit your people as well as mine."

"I would like to hear of this proposition," said Walks Silent, curious as to what his people could do for a white man who undoubtedly had so much more than they.

"It's a simple plan," explained Caleb. "It has been a good year for the farms of Matt and myself. We have much in the way of food and other provisions, far more than we will need to survive the winter. I also have hundreds of acres of land, most of which I intend to leave untouched. However, there are many other acres I would like to clear of trees and rocks and use as farm land and pasture. It will take many strong men to do this work which is why I would ask the help of you and your people to clear the land."

"And in return?" asked Walks Silent hoping that his people would not be asked to work for the slave wages white men in Oklahoma customarily offered.

"In return I will pay your people with both money and land. For every five acres you clear, one acre of uncleared land will be deeded to the Cherokee and registered in the courthouse of Fannin County under whatever name you choose. The land will be owned by you and yours to do with as you wish. Also, for every four days a man works he will earn one dollar in hard money. Clothing and food will be provided for you and the building of shelter for your people will be our first task. That is my offer."

Hearing these words Walks Silent could barely fight back the emotions he was feeling as tears of hope and appreciation almost fell from his eyes.

"My heart smiles at your words," said Walks Silent, "and when would you have us begin?"

Two days later the Cherokee, three men, three women, and two children set up camp in a stand of woods between the Quinn and Moore homes.

It was as Caleb knew it would be. Christine and Samantha welcomed the Indians with open arms and formed an instant bond with the women and children. With no argument from their husbands or the Cherokee men, they immediately moved the women and children out of their tents and into the Quinn home until a more permanent and warmer shelter could be built for them.

Within a day the house was filled with the chatter and laughter of happy women and children, usually including Samantha and her daughters Eryn and Emmilou who showed absolutely no fear of the Cherokee and were even prone to using the laughing Cherokee warriors to play "piggy back" as they raced around the yard.

The Cherokee men were invited to stay with Matt and Samantha, but preferring to be nearer their families, kept their camp in the woods between the two families' farms.

During the next week while the women sewed new clothes for everyone, the men went out each day and felled the trees needed to construct a home for the Cherokee. Under Matt's expert and watchful eye, carefully selected trees were felled by axe, trimmed of their branches, and then dragged by mule or teams of horses to the building site. There logs were measured, skinned of their bark, cut, squared, smoothed and notched with a large-handled drawing knife, making them ready to be turned into an Appalachian-style log home spacious enough to comfortably hold all eight of the Cherokee. Matt, himself, built the cavernous fireplace that would serve for cooking and heating the house.

Five days before Thanksgiving, Caleb, Matt, and the Cherokee laid the last floorboard in the new home where Walks Silent and his people would live. To the front of the house flowed a clear creek while the rear of the Cherokee property was adjacent to the hundreds of acres Caleb had set aside "to go untouched forever."

The location was ideal for the growing of crops in front of the house, while the woods to the rear provided an abundance of game and protection from the winter winds. It was also as Caleb assured them, "land the railroads and timber companies would never touch."

It was a day of hope and immense pride for the Cherokee and their new neighbors the Moore and Quinn families.

Chapter 7
The New South

Under a white cloud of steam belching from the locomotive, the combination ore and passenger train chugged out of the Tennessee mining town of Copper Hill shortly before noon, giving Beau and Phillip a first hand look at what only a decade or so before had been pristine mountain country filled with dense trees and clear flowing rivers and streams. It was now a land stripped of all but a few trees, its rivers filled with debris of all sorts, a wasted, watery junk yard for man's many leftovers. It was typical of the mining towns sprouting throughout the mountains and valleys of the Appalachians.

"That," remarked Phillip to the much smaller man sitting across from him, "was one ugly town."

"It was that and more," replied Beau as he gazed out the window at the passing countryside, "and a sad reminder of what man can accomplish in only a few short years, all in the name of progress."

"I wouldn't call it progress," Phillip replied. "I'd call it what happens when the men owning the mining companies buy or lease the land for almost nothing, rape it of everything of value, and then move on. They don't give a damn about anything but the almighty dollar."

Never missing a chance to play the Devil's Advocate to his large friend's positions on the state of the world, Beau shot back, "I was being facetious but you could think of it this way…because of man's march to progress we are now sitting here in a fairly comfortable and fast moving passenger car as opposed to traveling by some primitive and painful means of conveyance such as a horse or horse drawn buggy. Both means of conveyance are practically guaranteed to render our hind quarters sore and miserable. My only consolation is that you of the more than ample posterior, would be suffering more than I."

As usual, Beau had left his friend little room for argument, so Phillip retreated to what he did best.

"Wake me up when we get to our stop," said Phillip after pulling his hat over his eyes and leaning his head against the train's window.

Less than a half hour later and under a bright noon day sun a squinting Beau and Phillip set their feet on the reddish colored soil of Mineral Bluff, Georgia.

"If you'll watch our bags I'll check with the station master about renting a buggy, if that's possible in this hot bed of advanced civilization."

The prospect of riding a hard-seated buggy, much less a horse, already had Beau in a cranky frame of mind.

Phillip watched as Beau entered the brick train depot from the rear and then emerged a minute later out the front entrance, crossed the road and disappeared around the corner of a building with a sign on it that read Binder's General Store. Beau's disappearance in the small town didn't particularly worry Phillip because Beau, although looking like a mild-mannered lawyer or business man, was well equipped to handle himself in almost any scrap. Still, they were in Georgia, and Georgia was part of the southern culture marking them as outsiders, outsiders who might draw trouble from anywhere at any time. The trouble wasn't long in coming.

Three men riding on a freight wagon loaded with wooden crates carrying chickens and geese brought their wagon to a stop in front of the general store, climbed down and were starting to unload their cackling freight when they noticed the well-dressed black man standing across the road from them. Out of the corner of his eye Phillip watched as the men stopped their work and gestured with their hands and eyes in his direction.

"Yeah," thought Phillip, "lucky me is about to get a dose of real southern hospitality."

Phillip quickly analyzed the men and their potential threat to his welfare. One of them was short and stocky with a bull neck, a large belly, and a badly pock-marked face. A second man was tall and thin with long arms and a weasel-looking face dominated by a long pointed nose. Neither looked particularly dangerous, just the typical overall-wearing working sons of the South. It was the third man on whom Phillip focused his greater attention. He was huge, going well over 300 pounds and inches past six feet in height. He had a shabby-looking red beard and even the loose fitting heavy shirt he wore under his dirty overalls couldn't hide the outline of his well-muscled arms and shoulders.

It was red beard, who speaking loudly enough for Phillip to hear, told the other two, "Looks like we got us a fancy dressed nigger in town."

The words coming from his mouth were followed by a long stream of tobacco spit intentionally aimed in Phillip's direction.

The shorter of the men casually placed his hand on red beard's shoulder and announced, "I think we should show him what men what fought with Bobby Lee think of all them 'freed' niggers."

After an exchange of glances between them, the men spread out three across and headed toward Phillip, confident in their numbers and sure they were about to teach another deserving black man a hard and bloody lesson in the ways of Georgia mountain life.

Unperturbed, Phillip stared at the men as they made their way toward him, giving them a cold look from his ebony eyes that said, "I dare you."

He stood straight and relaxed as the three men stopped only an arm's reach in front of him. He knew they intended to do him serious harm, but like most bullies it was unlikely they would do anything until they built up their courage by shooting off their mouths. Men such as these were not new to Phillip and in most cases not to be abided. This was one such case.

"Boy," said the tall skinny man as they came to a stop in front of him, "wha'cha doin' standin' in our way?"

Phillip looked the speaker in the face but made no reply.

"We're talkin' to ya boy," added red beard as he stepped within arm's reach. "Ya hear me talking to ya, boy?"

He then moved a few inches closer and stared into Phillip's face, expecting, that as usual, any black man he confronted would either back up, move aside, or better yet, even start apologizing for being in his way. He hardly saw what happened next.

Phillip's fist struck the red-bearded man square in the middle of his face, breaking his nose and sending him reeling backwards until he landed hard on the seat of his overalls with his legs pointing at the sky.

Even before red beard hit the dirt Phillip was stepping to his left and sending a vicious and closed-fist backhand to the side of weasel-face's head, a blow that struck him just above the ear. The man slumped to the ground, out of the fight and more than half unconscious.

Pock-marked then sent a hard-toed boot at Phillip's groin, hoping to bring the black man to his knees and render him defenseless. What he got for his effort was his leg being held high in the air by the ankle. He was still jumping on his one free leg when he heard "wrong move," and then saw, but couldn't avoid, the fist that struck him flush in the mouth, splitting both his lips and pushing three of his front teeth out of their sockets.

Phillip released the bleeding man in time to meet a now upright red beard's charge, an action which brought the two men chest-to-chest and face-to-face like two bulls squaring off against each other. Phillip did not resist when the man's muscled arms wrapped around him, pinning Phillip's arms to his side. Red beard had used this same "bear hug" a countless number of times before to break the backs of his opponents, black, white, or Indian. Clasping the fingers of his hands together he began to squeeze with all his strength, expecting to force the air out of Phillip's lungs, to bend him backward, and then to end the contest by snapping the man's back. Despite his best effort, nothing he expected to happen happened.

The black man in his grasp simply stood there unmoving and seemingly unfazed, with his arms relaxed at his sides. Quickly shifting his grip further down on Phillip's back red beard tried again, and once again the black man stood with his back unbent, as if made of stone.

For the first time in his adult life red beard began to feel a sense of panic.

A surprisingly soft voice then whispered in his ear, "You lose."

Red beard now felt steely arms wrapped around his back, the knuckles of clasped iron hands beginning to press into his spine, forcing him to arch his back, to fight for a breath, to replace the air being slowly squeezed from his lungs. With a fast ebbing strength he fought back, bending his knees, jerking his hips and shoulders back and forth, trying every trick he knew to break the hold. To his horror the arms continued squeezing, forcing more air from his lungs, and bringing his ribs to the breaking point. He looked into the face of the black man. Cold eyes stared calmly back at him as if he was nothing more than a small nuisance.

Uttering two words he had never spoken to any other man except the father who had taught him how to fight and how to maim, he blurted out, "I give."

Red beard felt the arms holding him go slack, allowing him the chance to suck a great gasp of precious air into his burning lungs. He then collapsed to his knees. Through the ringing in his ears he heard the black man speak.

"Now that you've had your fun with this 'boy,' I suggest you and your piss-ant friends find something else to do because if any of you say another word to me I will continue where we left off."

A minute later the freight wagon carrying the three humiliated and thoroughly whipped men was making fast tracks out of town.

Chapter 8
The Reunion

Ten minutes after the wagon rolled out of Mineral Bluff, Beau returned driving a strange-looking black buggy with what looked like a long tall black box on it. It was being pulled by two ancient-looking white mules Phillip heard Beau refer to as "Jack and Jill."

Laughing at the sight, Phillip had to ask, "Is that a hearse or a traveling outhouse?"

"It is a hearse and a fine one at that…not to mention the only wheeled method of transportation available," replied Beau with a look of chagrin, "I just hope it's not an omen of things to come."

"Any trouble while I was gone?" he then asked.

"Nothing worth mentioning," replied Phillip while tossing their bags into the hearse and then jumping on to the driver's seat beside Beau, "but I do believe we should move along before some of the folks around here start thinking I'm a bit too uppity."

"Good idea," said Beau, and with a "giddy up" and a slap of the long reins to the rumps of the mules, headed the hearse toward the home of Caleb Quinn. Content at the moment to let Phillip define for himself what constituted trouble, Beau made no mention of the fresh drops of blood and scuffed up dirt he had seen on the ground where Phillip had been standing.

For the next two hours the men traveled through a landscape that even in winter was as beautiful as any they had ever seen. The land was rough and mostly thick with trees but where it had been cleared there were farms and log houses that any man would have been proud of, and in particular Phillip who had never truly had a home of his own, and would be very much at home in this rural area.

A mixture of sturdy horses and fat cattle were feeding on the hay stacks covering the pastures. Row upon row of dried up corn stalks left over from harvesting could be seen as further proof of the land's fertility.

An hour later when the carriage was within sight of a sign reading "North Carolina border" they left the main road, marked as the Murphy Road.

Beau turned the carriage to the right, following the curving road which was hardly more than shallow ruts caused by the passing of previous wagons. Set back to the left about a hundred yards away was a small cabin with smoke coming out of the chimney and a tattered Confederate flag nailed above the front door.

Phillip took a moment to comment on the other Confederate flags they had seen on display at many of the houses they had passed when leaving Mineral Bluff.

"Lots of flags flying in these parts," he told Beau.

"I noticed," replied Beau, "lots of good flag-loving people around here."

"Maybe they don't know the war's over."

"They know it's over, they're just reluctant to admit they lost. I think the flags are just a reminder of the pride these people feel for the men and boys who fought and died for the South and for the state of Georgia. You've got to admit, the South may have lacked a lot of material things necessary for fighting and winning a war, but men of courage wasn't one of them."

"Sounds like you kind of admire them."

"I do feel it speaks well of them that they fought so long and hard against what any man would deem impossible odds."

"I'll give them that," said Phillip, "but they fought for the wrong cause and I call that plain stupid."

"Still," said Beau, "if you look at it from their perspective they were fighting to preserve their homes, their culture, their way of life. The only way of life most of them had ever known. For that reason I'd call them misguided as opposed to either stupid or wrong."

"Yeah," said Phillip, "you believe fighting to preserve slavery is only a misguided notion?"

"It was a lot more complex than that," said Beau, knowing that for much of Phillip's life he had endured slavery up close and personal.

He also knew his friend, who had been separated at an early age from his parents, carried hidden scars left over from those years, and only a few of the scars were on the outside.

"The South needed slavery because of cotton; cotton the South exported to England at great profit to the plantation owners. In turn the South imported many of the goods they needed from England. This didn't sit well with the mill owners in the Northeast who wanted the South's cotton at cheap non-competitive prices and wanted the Southerners to buy their needed goods from the North rather than from England and other foreign countries. To achieve this end, Northern industrial leaders influenced the politicians in the North who outnumbered politicians in the South to pass into law high tariffs designed to cripple the South's trade with England."

"So," said Phillip, "your contention is greed, not slavery, got a half million men killed or wounded."

"Yes," said Beau. "Greed, pride, even the fine intentions of the anti-slavery people, all mixed together with a good measure of the stupidity you mentioned. They all fueled the fires that first split the country, and then brought it to the worst of man's accomplishments, civil war, brother killing brother, with each side claiming God's favor."

Phillip usually enjoyed hearing Beau's insightful way of explaining things, their "cause and effect" as Beau often put it, but not this time. Wanting to end the discussion he said, "Thanks for the history lesson but I've got another question for you."

"Go ahead," said Beau.

"You sure this is the way we want to go?"

Beau shot a quick glance to the front of them, seeing only trees that blocked his view as the rutted road curved shapely to the right.

"I'm just following the directions the livery owner gave me, and he told me to go right at the last turn before the North Carolina border. And besides, that looks like chimney smoke to me," he said, pointing ahead to the distant light grey smoke rising above the trees.

Minutes later the heavy woods they were traveling through opened up to reveal the best looking farm they had seen as of yet. The setting was a narrow curving valley running between the mountains. The almost level land was filled with neat rows of barren fruit trees and wild blackberry bushes and had a gentle creek flowing through it. A large pond was home to a great number of ducks and geese, some that looked wild and must have decided to winter there, and others which by their coloration were most likely domestic. A large red barn with several black and white milk cows standing around it sat in the middle of the property. At least five acres were filled with the now familiar rows of dried out corn stalks. A fenced pasture of about three acres was dotted with hay stacks and held a half dozen or so horses, four mares, a buckskin gelding, a painted pony, and a palomino stallion that looked up from his grazing and nickered what Beau took to be a greeting.

"That big boy is one beautiful horse," Phillip said to Beau, but speaking more to himself, not really caring whether his horse hating friend was listening or not.

"He's got to be the mustang stallion Caleb brought from Texas after his run-in with the Comanche."

"That's not the only beautiful thing he brought from Texas," replied Beau, referring to the tall blond-haired woman who had stepped out of the oblong Appalachian-style log home.

She was standing on the front porch and looking at them, shading her eyes with one hand and using the other hand to hold a black haired infant. To Beau's eye, he and Phillip had to be looking at Caleb's wife Christine and their son, Sean Michael.

"Good afternoon gentlemen," said Christine as the hearse was brought to a stop in front of the porch, "may I help you?"

"And a good afternoon to you, ma'am," answered the slender man in a suit sitting next to an imposing black man who, in size, could have been a physical match for Matt, if not even a few pounds and inches larger.

"Is it possible you could spare two hungry strangers a meal?"

Strangers weren't unsettling to her as they may have been to some women, but they rarely visited her secluded mountain valley. For her part she welcomed the occasional visitors because they often carried news from the outside to the isolated mountain homes and communities. However, it was very unusual, to say the least, for them to arrive driving a hearse.

"I'd be happy to do so, if you don't mind waiting until my husband gets…"

Before she spoke another word the realization of who these men were suddenly hit her. Stepping one step forward as she hitched the baby even further up in her arms and with a dazzling smile appearing on her face, she exclaimed, "You two are no strangers to this house and more than welcome. Lord knows Caleb has spoken so often and so highly of Beau Carroll and Phillip Buckner that you have always been considered part of our family."

Beau, who like Phillip, had no family of his own was deeply moved. Rising to a standing position he doffed his hat and swept it gracefully toward Christine.

"Never before," he said, as he placed a hand on Phillip's shoulder, "have we been so warmly greeted or more thankful for our friendship with your husband."

"Your being here honors both me and my home," said Christine, "and if you'll come inside I hope to repay your kind words with that meal you spoke of."

No mules were ever unhitched and set out to graze as fast as the two that had brought Beau and Phillip to their destination.

Chapter 9
The Plot Revealed

Later that evening, after eating a meal fit for kings, Caleb, Beau and Phillip, now together for the first time since after Lincoln's speech at Gettysburg, sat before the cavernous fireplace enjoying the warmth given off by crackling pine logs while sipping on mugs of scalding hot coffee doused with a touch of whiskey and honey.

"Your visit pleases me more than you can know," Caleb told his long-time friends, "however, coming as you did at this time of year makes me suspect it's not entirely a social call. But don't tell Christine you might be taking me away from her and Sean Michael or we'll all be eating cold earthworms for breakfast."

"In the interest of my great appreciation for your wife's cooking, my lips are sealed for now," said Beau. "But you're right about this being more than a social visit. There is a matter of great importance I came here to discuss with you."

The seriousness of Beau's words was matched by the solemn look Caleb saw on Phillip's face.

"Well," pondered Caleb, thinking of his family, "what I spoke of in jest about leaving them may well be a truth."

Looking back at Beau he said, "Tell me."

"To begin with," said Beau, "you must understand several key factors. The first of these being that this country is on the brink of bankruptcy. Our government borrowed an enormous amount of money to pay for the war and now our creditors, both foreign and domestic, are clamoring for repayment. These loans, as well as the greenbacks we put into circulation, are backed by government-owned gold, gold that is intended to guarantee our loans and the validity of our printed money."

Beau paused, gathering his thoughts and noted that Caleb was slightly nodding his head in understanding.

"What the public must not know is that our debt far exceeds our gold reserves. If they did know, it could lead to a nation-wide run on our banks by people demanding an exchange of their paper money for gold. If the run were accompanied by a similar demand by our major creditors, within weeks the treasury would be utterly depleted of its gold reserves, and that would most likely bring down the government."

"What you're telling me is that for the most part paper money, including yours and mine, is only as good as the confidence the public has in it?"

"Exactly," replied Beau, "lose that confidence and our printed money is nothing but paper, no better than the Confederate bills that weren't worth the paper they were printed on even before the end of the war."

After a slight delay to take a swallow of coffee and compose his next words, Beau continued.

"This then brings me to the next problem involving paper money. Throughout the South and Southwest, meaning most of the former Confederate states, private and state run banks and even cities can and have printed their own money. Their currency is backed by their own gold or silver. Unfortunately, it is estimated that up to thirty per cent or more of the privately printed notes in circulation are counterfeit or totally lacking any backing by either gold or silver. As such, they are basically worthless notes. This situation poses a threat of collapsing the banking institutions which circulate them. That in turn poses a serious threat to the Federal government's ability to distribute its currency."

"So, I take it you're here to get my help with the problems," said Caleb. "It sounds like a job for bureaucrats at the most and local law at the least. Not being the owner of a gold mine, I don't see anything I could do that they couldn't do."

"I'll get to that in a minute," said Beau, "but first let me continue with the rest of what I need you to know."

"Please do," replied Caleb, now growing anxious to know what his role in this drama would be.

"The President, whom I spoke with recently, feels the immediate threat to our currency and our government comes from Mexico. Before Juarez had Maximilian executed and supposedly ended France's influence in North America, we had strong suspicions that Maximilian and Napoleon III had forged a plan to inundate the United States, all the way from Maine to Louisiana to California, with counterfeit money. They intended to do, with worthless counterfeit currency, what they couldn't hope to do militarily or politically. Namely, bring down this government."

"By that you mean to once again make those lands you mentioned part of Mexico and therefore part of the French empire?"

"Your assessment of international politics is quite accurate," said Beau, "but now to the current problem."

"It is my belief and that of President Johnson that Juarez, in conjunction with die-hard Confederates, despite jailing General Pickett for thirty days when he went to Mexico seeking support for the Confederacy during the war, is continuing France's plan to fully discredit our monetary system and may have already implemented the first stages of the plan."

Caleb interrupted Beau once again, "It would seem that Juarez didn't like the French but liked at least one of their ideas. I take it he plans to reclaim what was first Spanish and then Mexican territory while the Confederates want to once again raise the rebel flag over the southern states."

"You have it correct," replied Beau, and then reached into his inner coat pocket and extracted two envelopes.

"Just this past week in Washington, Phillip took this envelope from a person bent on my demise," he said.

He then handed Caleb the large envelope containing counterfeit five and ten dollar greenbacks Phillip had taken from the dead assassin.

Caleb examined the money, all crisp new bills, and all tightly stacked. They looked legitimate. He then fanned the bills out in front of him looking for and finding the telltale identical serial numbers.

"Excuse me for a moment," said Caleb as he rose from the horse-hide covered chair and moved to a desk sitting in a corner where he opened a drawer and removed a crisp twenty dollar greenback from it.

"Weeks ago I got this bill from the bank in Murphy," he told his two guests.

Beau and Phillip remained quiet as Caleb held one of the bills given him by Beau and the one he had taken from the drawer in front of the fireplace and took several seconds to compare them.

"If you hadn't told me otherwise, except for the serial numbers I wouldn't have been able to tell which of the bills was counterfeit. They look and feel the same and the color of the ink is identical."

After another brief look at the bills he added, "Who can do this kind of work?"

"That my astute young friend is one of the three overlapping mysteries surrounding this money," answered Beau.

"And the other two mysteries?" asked Caleb.

"Secondly, and of immediate personal concern to me, is what could be the possible connection between the bogus money and someone being paid to kill me. That begs another question, and one that keeps me awake at night, namely, the place and timing of the attempt on my life. For that to have happened as it did just after my meeting with the President suggests that someone close to President Johnson confided to the shooter the time and place where I would exit a very secret tunnel that only a few select individuals know exists. As much as the informant might have endangered my life, the loss of that secrecy makes me far more concerned with the potential threat to the President himself. One plot to kill him by blowing up his train has already been uncovered. I fear that other attempts may be coming, perhaps from within the White House itself."

Then with a look of total commitment he added, "I've lost one President and don't intend to lose another if I can help it."

"I can't believe it's a coincidence," said Caleb. "Maybe it's something in your past, because if what I know of your activities over the years is even half true, you have earned your share of enemies…but that brings us back to the money."

"Yes, the money," said Beau, "or more to the point how to determine what's real, what's counterfeit, and perhaps more importantly, who's printing it and where. Start with this fact. The paper the government uses is produced at a secure facility in Philadelphia in a way so precise that any denomination of 454 bills will always weigh exactly one pound. The notes are then sent to the Bureau of Printing and Engraving for signing, cutting, and trimming. We are positive this process can not be duplicated."

"What if it could?" asked Caleb, thinking of the expertise his old friend Joshua Webster exhibited in producing the false legal documents which had allowed him to escape the English.

"Then, other than the duplicated numbers there would be little way for a person or a bank to detect large quantities of bogus bills."

"And what if someone could come up with a means of mass producing greenbacks without duplicating the numbers?"

"Then, metaphorically speaking," said Beau, "it would be lights out at the U.S. Bureau of Engraving and Printing in Washington DC. After that, the lights will go out in the White House. All this brings us back to the role we will play in order to stop any such conspiracy."

Beau opened the second envelope, removed a letter, and handed it to Caleb.

"I want you to carry this letter with you. You may not have any need of it but if you do, don't hesitate to use it."

Caleb opened the envelope to learn he was now a U.S. marshal and answerable only to the President of the United States.

"What?" asked a much impressed Caleb, "no oath?"

"As far as I'm concerned you took that oath when you stepped off the ship in Baltimore," replied Beau.

It was an answer he felt applied to both himself and Caleb.

Caleb was about to ask another question when Phillip stood up, moved to the front window, and asked a question of his own, "Caleb, are you expecting guests, maybe a lot of them?"

Chapter 10
Uninvited Guests

Caleb listened and could just barely hear the hoof beats from what sounded like a large number of galloping horses heading in the direction of the house.

"Renegades?" he asked himself, thinking of the Cherokee who had raided whites along the Nantahala.

He quickly dismissed this because it was highly unlikely renegade Indians would move in such large numbers and even less likely they would so loudly announce their arrival. If his second thought was correct the riders could be a far greater threat than any band of Indians.

Caleb moved to the front door, opened it, and looked out. What he saw moving in the darkness were burning torches coming toward the house. Suspicions confirmed, he turned to his guests.

"Gentlemen, I'm afraid we have some unexpected and unwelcome company."

Racing quickly to the bedroom door to check on Christine and Sean Michael, he opened the door just a few inches and peered into the room. Both of them were sound asleep. Closing the door softly and moving to the gun rack above the fireplace and out of a child's reach, he took down the Colt revolvers, the Sharps he had used during the war and again against the Comanche, his shotgun, and lastly, his Henry repeating rifle. Christine's shotgun was the only weapon left on the gun rack.

"Sharps, Henry, or shotgun?" he asked Phillip.

"The Sharps will make a good start,'" answered Phillip with no hesitation, "but I'll also be getting my old Navy revolver out of my luggage."

"Beau was already moving to where he and Phillip had dropped their bags when he heard Caleb ask, "Shotgun?"

"No thanks," said Beau, as he patted the cuffs of his sleeves, each of which concealed a Derringer. "I prefer something less conspicuous and capable of more than two shots, such as my little six shot Pepper Box."

He then reached into his bag and withdrew an oddly shaped pistol which had six revolving barrels.

"I've got to be close in for it to be effective, but I get around that by using my slight stature and innocent look to draw in whoever threatens me. Should my docile appearance fail to deter an attack, I'll have a total of six shots with which to defend myself."

Not bothering to argue the point, Caleb quickly blew out the single lamp illuminating the room, and with his two well-armed guests following him, went out on the front porch to meet the torch-bearing riders.

He was reasonably sure he knew why they were here. It had to be because of Phillip being in the house, not to mention the Cherokee now living on his property and the Quinn's Catholic faith. It was trouble he had hoped wouldn't materialize because it would set him against his neighbors.

Barely seconds later, the hooded horsemen numbering over a dozen, and all of them whooping and hollering, came to a halt in front of the house.

Caleb understood the reasons for their hollering; first to intimidate, and secondly to expel some of their nervousness while at the same time building up their courage. It was the same courage building yells Rebel infantrymen and cavalry let out as they charged into battle. He also knew the hollering usually worked, and was a likely prelude to a full scale attack on his home.

Caleb stepped out on the porch and braced himself, ready for anything and certain that Phillip and Beau, standing behind him and on either side, were ready to spill blood if that's what it came down to.

Nervous moments passed while the riders, their heads covered by burlap bags or white cloth sacks, took the time to evaluate the men on the porch. They could see two men with rifles, Caleb Quinn and a black man who was half hidden in the dark. The third and much smaller man on the porch was not visibly armed and seemed to be harmless.

After a scant few seconds had passed one of the lead riders moved to the front of the group and then swung his mount sideways to the porch.

Caleb raised his left hand and pointed it palm out at the rider.

"You're not welcome here," he said in a voice that easily carried to all the riders.

"We ain't har lookin' for no welcome," came back the reply from the horseman. "We're har 'cause y'all got thievin' Injuns livin' on yar'n property and a nigger and Yankee sum'bitch under yar'n roof. We're fixin' to change that so you best git out of our way."

"They are my guests," replied Caleb in a voice clearly indicating the two men wouldn't be given over without gun play.

"That nigger ain't no guest and don't belong under a white man's roof."

Another voice spoke up, "Ya tell 'im!"

Caleb was sure he recognized the second voice as belonging to a neighbor boy who lived with his widowed mother only a few miles away, a boy left fatherless by the war. A boy of fourteen or fifteen Caleb had given work during the summer past, work that didn't really need doing.

"Johnny," Caleb replied in a soft measured tone, "the man being spoken of is a good man, the kind of man I hope you live long enough to become."

"We come for the nigger," shouted another man from the very rear of the group.

A second later a rope formed into a noose came out of the darkness and landed in the dirt just short of the porch.

"That's for yur guest," shouted another voice.

"Give 'im over now," said another rider from out of the darkness, "or we'll take 'im and burn ya to the ground."

Caleb realized the situation was about to go from bad to worse and a peaceful resolution was getting more and more unlikely. Faced by only three men against their dozen or more, the riders were feeling a growing confidence.

Switching the Henry rifle from his right hand to his left Caleb then placed his right hand on the handle of his revolver. Although the Henry would be more intimidating, at such close range the six-shot revolver would be more effective firing into a closely bunched group of men on horseback. He waited, expecting the dying to start at any second. He could never have anticipated the event to come.

From behind him a shotgun blast sent a hail of pellets into the ground below the belly of the roan mare ridden by the horsemen's leader. The result was immediate and somewhat spectacular.

The mare lowered her head, arched her back and then went airborne, throwing her rider backward onto her hindquarters. Jarring the ground and rider with her landing, she again threw her head down and her hindquarters skyward, launching the hooded rider high into the night air. After what seemed like an impossible amount of gravity-defying time to be airborne, the rider landed shoulders first on the hard packed ground. The shotgun blast, seemingly coming out of nowhere, also caused the groups of men, both those on horseback and those on the porch, to freeze in place.

Christine had fired the shot exactly where she intended and got exactly the effect she wanted. She then attempted to slip forward from her position just inside the doorway of the house but was blocked from doing so by Caleb's firm right arm.

"No," she told him without taking her eyes off the hooded man sprawled in the dirt, "I've got something to say that these men need to hear."

Caleb, now aware the stunned riders, to a man, were sitting quiet and motionless, lowered his arm allowing Christine to move past him and to the front of the porch.

With her temper at its fullest because of the threats made to her home and family, and with a still smoking shotgun in her hand, she looked at the fallen rider and in a voice which was all threat addressed the men.

"I have another barrel full of buckshot and I'll use it if you don't get off our property now!"

The riders had come to intimidate, not get bloody, and were now confronted by an angry woman with a shot gun. They believed her words, saw her temper, and instantly began to reconsider their situation.

Christine continued, "You men can wear hoods over your heads but I still know most of you."

"Shane Howell," she said as she pointed the shotgun toward a man at the front,

"I've been to your house teaching your kids their numbers. And now you come here to threaten my family? I gave you credit for being a better man than that."

"And you," she said to a man riding bareback on a scrawny mule, "everyone knows you as Uncle Harrell and you and your daughter have set at my table more than once, and glad I was to have you because you've always been a gentleman and a good neighbor."

Then lowering the barrel of the shotgun she pointed to a lanky figure on a paint horse, "You there, Tom Redder, you can hide your face but I'd know your horse anywhere. And that fellow on your right is your cousin and supposedly a man of the cloth."

Swinging the shotgun to the right she addressed another man, "Walt Jacobs, I've bought chickens from you and I count you and your wife as good friends, and now you'd do us harm?"

Passion rising in her voice she continued speaking to the now subdued riders, "We've always been loyal neighbors. You are our friends. We trade with you, Caleb hires on locals whenever he can, I help to nurse your sick. We depend on each other…" her voice died off as a sob started to overcome her.

Losing the anger in her voice but not her determination, she continued, "When did people around here start showing strangers anything but the finest of hospitality?"

Even with the hood over his head it was apparent the man Christine identified as Shane Howell had lowered his head in shame.

Once again the young boy spoke up, "But Miz Christine, that thar's a black man."

"Yes, he is," replied Christine, "and my husband has already expressed our opinion of him. He's also a friend of ours and I'll not see any harm come to him."

Caleb, judging the time to intercede had arrived, stepped off the porch and helped the downed rider to his feet.

Speaking loudly he told him, "I suggest you and your friends leave now and don't come back unless it's in a friendly way."

"I'd do what he says," said a voice from behind the riders.

A figure casually carrying a shotgun over his shoulder then stepped out of the darkness and slowly walked between the riders until he reached the porch.

It was Matthew Moore, a man known by most of the riders as someone you angered at your own peril, a man whose fist could bring painful retribution if you wronged him, his family or his friends.

"Ya sidin' against us, against your own people Matt?" questioned a man in the middle of the group.

"I am and so are my friends who came with me, and I might remind you, the Quinns are also 'our people'" replied Matt.

His words were supported by the sound of men whistling bird noises in the dark from positions on either side of the riders.

"What y'all are hearing are the Cherokee "thieves" ya poor-mouthed. They are armed and they don't like being spoken ill of."

A minute later the hooded riders, not wanting to face unseen and unknown numbers of armed men on two sides, and armed men and a shotgun wielding woman in front of them, turned their horses away from the house and disappeared into the night.

Chapter 11
The Counter-Plan

An hour before sunrise the next morning Beau, Phillip, and Caleb ate a breakfast hot off Christine's prized wood-burning stove while they discussed what was to come.

"Do you mind if I listen in?" asked Christine, knowing there was little she wouldn't be able to hear even if the answer were "No."

It was Beau who answered, "I don't mind and in fact I welcome it because what President Johnson and I are asking of your husband is relevant to you in many ways. It will take Caleb away from you and your son for some time and could put him into a considerable degree of danger."

Beau then turned to Caleb, "I would like to begin with something of a history lesson so that we can catch Christine up on what we talked about yesterday evening."

"At the end of the war the monetary system in the Confederate states was in total disarray. Confederate money was worthless and our own Federal money was months away from distribution in the South. This left a huge void in the South which now was faced with little more than a barter economy. Fortunately a lot of privately controlled banks and some cities resolved the problem by printing up their own paper currency backed by their own gold and silver. This worked reasonably well at first but then the counterfeiters got busy. Most of the privately printed bills were simplistic in design, often being printed on one side only, which meant even amateurish counterfeiters could make reasonable duplicates of them. As a result it is estimated that over thirty per cent of the bills now in circulation in the southern states are bogus."

"Which leaves gold or silver as the only form of money that can truly be trusted," piped in Christine, thinking of the jar of gold and silver coins she had hidden in the pantry.

"Even coinage has not escaped the artistic endeavors of counterfeiters," replied Beau, "but that is of little consequence in comparison to the counterfeit paper money being put into circulation. All of which brings me to the reason for my being here."

"I take it we've come to the end of the history lesson?" questioned Christine.

"You are correct," replied Beau. "Now for the problem as it exists today."

"Excuse me," said Christine as a baby's cry came from the bedroom, "but a problem of a more immediate nature has awakened. I think something little needs a diaper change and some breakfast, but please continue while I tend to Sean Michael."

"A baby should always come before any discussion about the financial world," said Beau in all seriousness. "I'll do my best to speak loudly enough for you to hear while you attend to your son's needs."

After sipping from his coffee cup, Beau, repeating for Christine's benefit much of what had been spoken of the night before, continued. "As long as the counterfeiting was done on a local basis and mostly affected the currency issued by local banks, it was not a major problem to the government. However, for the last six months or so a disturbing change has been occurring. Counterfeit federal greenbacks are starting to show up in ever greater numbers. The distribution of this recent wave of counterfeiting seems to be originating in New Orleans and Galveston. We also have reliable information coming from several government agents, along with my own sources, that there is an active plan by the Mexican government to flood the country with counterfeit federal greenbacks of every denomination. As best we know, this international conspiracy began during the time Maximilian and France had control of Mexico. France's control of Mexico ended when Juarez stood Maximilian in front of a firing squad, but unfortunately the plan lived on through Juarez, meaning the current Mexican government. We now believe Juarez means to use counterfeit money to weaken our government to the extent that he will be able to take back the parts of North America once held by the Spanish and then Mexico."

"You mean Texas and California?" shouted Christine from the bedroom.

"And more," answered Beau.

"It sounds like Juarez may be biting off more than he can chew," said Caleb.

"Not necessarily," cut in Beau. "Juarez could be supported by die-hard Confederates who want to resurrect the south. These men, and there are hundreds of them with some in well-placed political offices, if joined with Juarez, would make a formidable threat. They are an enemy that has yet to show its face, but it is our job to reveal that face."

"And the plan is…?" asked Caleb.

"The best plan I can come up with based on the limited information I have is this. Phillip and I will go to New Orleans and with luck meet up with an agent of the Secret Service there. By the way, Lucinda is also in New Orleans and with her connections might be a providential ally as we try to find the counterfeiters. I have reason to suspect it's the same people who printed money for the Confederacy during the war and who now are operating out of the two cities I mentioned. However, that is just an educated guess and far from a certainty. Whatever the case, the men behind the plot must be caught or otherwise rendered harmless using whatever means are necessary."

Caleb was momentarily caught up in memories of his old friend, Lucinda Baker, and her escapades in New Orleans during her youth. His reminiscing was interrupted by Beau's voice.

"Caleb, if the men we're seeking aren't operating out of New Orleans they may be in Galveston or even Austin. Galveston, like New Orleans, is a hub of commerce, the largest city in Texas and a seaport. It's the most logical distribution point in Texas. But during the last part of the war when Galveston was taken by the Union, the Confederates were rumored to have hidden their printing machinery somewhere, either on the island, or, possibly, as far west as Austin. It's all speculation at this point but the trail of counterfeit greenbacks does appear to definitely lead to both New Orleans and Galveston. Counterfeiting has been a problem in many cities, but even more so in New Orleans. For several years New Orleans printed demand notes of its own but so many of the notes in circulation were counterfeit the city was forced to shut down the printing of its personalized money."

"It sounds as if we'll be calling on anybody with access to a printing machine," said Caleb.

"But we're not just looking for a printing operation," continued Beau.

"The men behind this scheme may be sitting on a lot of the gold and silver the Confederates were thought by some to have stockpiled toward the end of the war. Speculation is a large amount of gold and silver may be hidden somewhere in the hill country around Austin but, like I said, it's only speculation."

"So there are at least two proverbial needles in the haystack to search for," said Caleb, "one would be finding the gold and silver; the other would be learning the locations of the printing operations."

"Well put," said Beau, "We suspect the man we need to find first may be a master engraver and a printer. It's likely he's part of the conspiracy. His name is John Finley. We're not sure, but there is some evidence he made the plates the Confederacy used to print their money, and after the war did the same for private banks. Unfortunately, it seems he has disappeared, vanished into thin air."

"Any description or pictures of him?" asked Caleb.

"No pictures and only a sketchy description. He's been described by people who knew him as tall, slender but well-muscled, with straight dark hair, and in his early forties. They also said he wears glasses at all times and has never been able to completely rid himself of the ink on his hands. That's something to look for when you get to Galveston."

"Does he have any family?"

"Perhaps a brother, but we can't confirm that because so many records were lost or deliberately destroyed near the end of the war. Phillip and I will be going to New Orleans, which means I need you to begin your search in Texas as soon as you can make arrangements."

That shouldn't take long," said Caleb. "I travel light."

Knowing he was sending Caleb on a journey he might not return from, Beau replied, "Please, why don't you and Christine take whatever time you need to figure out how she will handle things while you're gone. In the meantime Phillip and I will go outside for a breath of fresh air."

After Beau and Phillip left the house, Caleb and Christine formulated a plan that would work to their best advantage. They were aided in their planning by Matt who had just dropped in to see if a second breakfast was available for his ever empty stomach. Looking for breakfast was also his excuse for making sure no other trouble was hounding his friends.

****

Several hours later, the sun had burned away the morning mist and replaced it with an azure blue sky as Caleb, Beau, and Phillip made their way on horseback over the summit of My Mountain. Due to its steep ruggedness it was a little used trail into Blue Ridge, but by taking it they avoided going through Mineral Bluff and a possible encounter with some of their visitors from the previous evening. The two mules and the hearse were left behind for their owner to find.

"Phillip," said Beau as he attempted to make an adjustment in the saddle and ease his already sore buttocks, "if you'd had the decency to tell me of your encounter with your three Southern friends outside the railroad station I might now be sitting in a somewhat more comfortable buggy as opposed to this torturous saddle."

"My apologies," said Phillip, "but wasn't it your buddy at the livery who must have told last night's visitors where to find us?"

"I stand corrected," replied Beau with mocking sincerity.

After yet another adjustment to his posterior he asked Caleb, "How much longer must I suffer until we reach our destination?"

"Once we cross the summit, go through Blue Ridge, and then get to the station in Ellijay, you'll be on the train to Atlanta in two to three hours," Caleb told him.

For the next half hour the men rode in silence until Phillip asked Caleb, "What about your family while you're gone? I hate to think we brought trouble to them or that last night's visitors might return without you being there."

"Christine and I have settled on a solution which keeps trouble away while at the same time keeping the family together as much as possible."

"And that solution would be?"

"Christine has family near Austin and we figure she and Sean Michael could stay with them while I look around Galveston and Austin. We'll go out there together and then I'll go on to Galveston alone."

"You could be gone for months, so what happens to your place while you're away?" asked Phillip.

He didn't say it, but he was worried the men from the night before might take advantage of Caleb's absence and raid the place.

"Not much to do around here during the winter but take care of the livestock, and Matt and the Cherokee will handle that for us. Besides that, I plan to have a Confederate flag flying high off the rooftop the entire time we're away. Matt tells me that between flying the flag and him and the Cherokee being nearby, it's all I need to do to keep the place safe. While the flag flying might sound like another of Matt's sick jokes, I'm not sure it is."

"Only in Georgia," said Phillip, as he laughed at the prospect of a Confederate flag protecting the home of someone who was a hero of the Union.

Phillip's laughter was interrupted by Beau. "There is one other thing to consider," he said looking at Caleb.

"According to the President we have no reliable source of intelligence coming out of Mexico. As such, we are blind in that area. I suggest, if it's at all possible, that your first endeavor be finding someone who can act as our eyes and ears south of the border."

Hearing Beau's words, Caleb's thoughts immediately jumped to the image of the Mexican gunfighter and sometimes outlaw, Dos Baca. His connections along the border, combined with his high level of intelligence and fighting skills, would make him perfect for the job. The only drawback with Dos was that given his tragic history with the Anglos in Texas the gunman might be more inclined to side with the Mexican government than that of the United States.

"I can think of one man who could do the job splendidly, if he wants to," said Caleb, "but he may not want to."

"And that man would be?" asked Beau.

80

"Someone who will remain known only to me and answerable only to me," replied Caleb.

Caleb's refusal to name the man brought a knowing grin to Beau's face and an even larger one to that of Phillip.

"Beau, I guess you've met your match when it comes to keeping a secret," said Phillip as he reached over and gave Beau a condescending pat on the shoulder.

Beau's only response was to press his heels into his horse's sides to encourage it to move a little faster.

Two hours later Beau and Phillip waved good-bye to Caleb as their train bound for Atlanta pulled out of the Ellijay station.

The following day Caleb, Christine, and little Sean boarded the same train on their way to Texas.

Chapter 12
An Unexpected Greeting

A gust of damp wind blowing from the north greeted Caleb as for the second time in his life he found himself getting off the stage coach in the Texas hill country town of Liberty Hill. He was reaching back inside the stage to help Christine with Sean Michael when a Mexican boy of thirteen or fourteen, sombrero in hand, approached them.

"You are Señor Caleb?" the boy asked as he ran the straw sombrero through his fingers.

"Yes," answered a puzzled Caleb.

The boy's presence, and not that of Tip or Ann, wasn't a good omen.

"I am Victor Rodriquez, and Señor Tip has told me to tell you there is trouble at the rancho and that he and Señora Ann can not be here to meet you."

"What kind of trouble?" Christine asked before Caleb could say anything.

"Very big trouble," said Victor. "Bad men, many of them, they come to the rancho. Señor Tip say they want the horses and cattle."

Caleb was looking at Christine when he asked Victor, "When did the trouble start?"

"I see the bad men this morning as I ride to the rancho to ask for work. There were six of them, maybe seven, Señor. The direction they were riding was to the north of the rancho where the cattle and horses are kept. I hid from them and then rode toward the rancho but before I get there I met my friend Dos and Señorita Shannon and Señor Tip and Señora Ann. They were coming to meet you, but when I tell them what I see, they send me to meet you. Then they go back to the rancho."

While Victor was talking, Caleb had been untying several pieces of luggage from the rear of the stage. The last piece was a black gun case held closed by two inch-thick leather straps. While he undid the straps he asked Victor, "And then what?"

"Then I come here to find you, like Señor Tip say."

As Caleb was listening, he removed the Henry rifle from the case, along with a matched pair of Colt 1860-issue army revolvers. It took him only seconds to make sure the weapons were loaded. The last things he removed from the gun case were several boxes of ammunition.

"Have you told the sheriff?"

"He is not here, so I tell Señor Rags what happened. He is very worried so he give me a horse to give to you, then he went to find the sheriff. Señor Rags, he say you will need a good horse, Señor."

Caleb looked at the lone horse tied to a hitching post only a dozen or so paces away. It was a big dappled gray gelding with a large scar on its forehead and a look in its eyes that promised a kick to anyone getting within range of its hind legs. The horse had a big head and was ugly enough that some people might have referred to it as a 'knothead.' On its back was a well-worn high pummeled Mexican-style saddle.

"Caleb," said Christine over the sound of Sean's vocal objection to the blowing wind hitting his eyes, "You know what you need to do, so don't worry about me and Sean Michael. We'll wait at the hotel with Victor until you come to get us."

Caleb knew his wife well enough to feel sure that she'd rather ride into trouble than wait for it to come to her. Were it not for Sean needing her care, he would have undoubtedly found himself on the wrong side of an argument if he had dared suggest she stay back and out of harm's way.

After a quick kiss to Christine and Sean and an "I love you" to both, Caleb was in the saddle and riding hard out of town.

To Caleb's surprise the gray was fresh, fast, and loved to run; so much so that several times Caleb was forced to rein him in ever so slightly. As much as he wanted to get to the ranch in the least amount of time, it wouldn't be good if he got there on a wind-busted horse, not if there was a chance the gray still had some running to do after they got to the house. Less than three hours later he jerked the gray to a dust-tossing stop as Ann, Shannon, and Gram, rifles in hand, poured out of the house to meet him. Ann was the first to speak.

"Good to see you, Caleb, and you got here just in the nick of time 'cause I figure Dos and Tip can use some help."

"Tell me what's happening," said Caleb, knowing there was no time for the usual courtesies.

"After we heard about the rustlers from Victor, we got back here and Tip and Dos grabbed some rifles and lit out. Their horses came back an hour later and that worried us some, but we've been hearing some shots off and on coming from the north so our men are still alive and fighting."

"Good," said Caleb, and started to turn the gray in the direction of the canyon, but found his way blocked by Shannon.

Reaching up, she gave him a cup of water which Caleb took the time to swallow down. It meant using up a few seconds of precious time, but he'd had nothing to drink since early morning and there was no telling when he'd get another chance.

With a "Thank you" to Shannon and a "Don't worry" to them all, he kicked the gray in the sides and headed for the box canyon.

Now he let the big horse have its head, and marveled that the animal was still able to run full out after the fast pace he'd maintained for over two hours. The grey, he realized, gelding or not, was one of only a few horses that might have been able to match his Palomino when it came to speed and stamina.

"Rags, you sure gave me the right horse for the job," he told himself.

He was still almost a half mile from the canyon when he heard the sound of a volley of shots, some of them the distinct pop of pistols, and the rest coming from what sounded like Winchesters.

Caleb tried to figure out what the shots were telling him, and it was more than just the fact that Tip and Dos were alive. For the fight to have lasted this long Tip and Dos must have had the good luck to corner the rustlers in the canyon. The box canyon, he remembered, was open on the south end and about a half mile further down came to a bottle-neck about forty or fifty yard across. From there the trail led slightly downward through a ravine that suddenly opened up to reveal a pasture land that was at least a half mile wide and a mile or so long before coming to an end against sheer fifty foot high walls. The neck of the canyon was the choke point Tip and Dos would have exploited if they had gotten there in time to do so. With it being so narrow across, it was the one place two well armed men had a chance of holding off the rustlers.

When horse and rider neared the mouth of the ravine, Caleb could see two figures exchanging gunfire with unseen gunmen firing from within the gap. Caleb led the horse to the right staying in the rocky cover offered as the terrain began to form the bottle-neck. After dropping the reins over the gray's head and trusting the horse was ground broke, he leapt from the saddle and ran with the saddlebag containing the extra ammunition in one hand and his Henry in the other while hollering out, "Tip, Dos, I'm coming in."

His voice rang throughout the canyon and mixed in with the louder echoes from the shots being fired. A bullet buzzing by his ear told him his arrival had not gone unnoticed by the rustlers in the northern part of the canyon.

Tip and Dos had taken cover behind a two foot high rock and dirt-lined embankment created by the small stream that ran year long out of the canyon and pooled at the entrance to the ravine.

Caleb headed for his friends on a dead run, zigzagging as he ran but not bothering to stay low. It was a moment that called for speed over caution. A minute later he splashed through the inch-deep water and slid to a wet stop between Tip and Dos. For an unexplained reason his arrival brought all the shooting to a stop.

"Good to see you two alive. Can I help out or is this a private party?" Caleb asked as matter-of-factly as he could.

"Well," Tip drawled, "with the horses run off we couldn't make our usual two-man cavalry charge and we couldn't retreat. We might a gone charging all them guns on foot but that didn't seem the smart thing to do, and retreating would have meant being caught in the open on foot, and I prefer, if I'm going to meet my Maker, to do it in bed. So, me and Dos figured our best bet was to stay here, hold the rustlers back in the canyon, and hope somebody heroic, like you, would come to the rescue before we ran out of ammunition."

Caleb had already noticed both men had holsters with empty loops where cartridges could usually be found.

"How close are you to being out?" he asked.

"I've got three rounds," said Tip.

"I have the same," said Dos, speaking for the first time.

Caleb looked at the pistols and rifles Tip and Dos were using. He didn't have any ammunition that would fit them.

"Take my Colts," he told them handing one pistol to Tip and tossing the other to Dos.

"Gracias, mi amigo," said Dos as he snatched the Colt out of the air.

"Ammo?" asked Tip.

"There are plenty of cartridges for the Colts in the saddlebag. We should have more than enough for what's coming."

Caleb dipped his hand into the right hand pocket of the saddlebag and then drew it out, cartridges spilling from his upturned palm. He handed them to Tip and then tossed the saddlebag to Dos.

"And you?" Dos asked.

"I'll use the Henry to take care of the long range shooting. You and Tip can back me up when they get in close."

"How do you figure they'll play it?" asked Tip, remembering that Caleb had an unusual ability to improvise a workable battle plan.

"Before I got here they probably figured they could wait you out until you ran out of bullets or simply pick you off at their leisure. Now that I'm here they're probably figuring there could be more help on the way, so my guess is they're getting ready to come out and hit us fast and hard."

"I'm thinking what you're thinking," said Tip.

"Yes," cut in Dos, "now that Caleb is here they will figure if one man comes others will follow."

As his friends spoke Caleb took a closer look at them, not liking what he saw. A steady stream of blood ran down Tip's neck from a nasty-looking gash just below his right ear.

"Looks like you got nicked a little," commented Caleb.

"A little," replied Tip, "but Dos there got the worst of it."

Caleb turned his eyes to the Mexican gunman and sometimes bandit. A large crimson stain covered his shirt on the lower left side under his vest. Much of the blood was already dry but a few drops were falling onto Dos' empty gun belt.

"How bad, amigo?"

Dos attempted to hide the grimace on his face as he stoically answered, "Caught a ricochet in the ribs but I will be ready when they come."

He did not mention a bullet had taken out a good sized piece of flesh just above his left collarbone.

Caleb studied Dos' face looking for a lie in his words. Dos was pale and jaw muscles were working against the pain. He had to be badly hurt, but Caleb also had little doubt that hurt bad or not, Dos was even more dangerous when wounded or cornered.

"Good to…."

Before Caleb could finish the sound of running horses approaching the gap from the north reached their ears.

Chapter 13
Rousting Rustlers

"Here they come," shouted Tip.

A second later the three men scrambled to take up firing positions behind the embankment and were ready as twenty or so riderless horses thundered out of the gap on a full run.

"Hold your fire," shouted Caleb over the noise of the horses' hooves and the sound of shots being used to drive them along.

As the horses broke through the gap they spread out slightly and then came straight at the men lying in the creek bed. Caleb looked past the horses and counted seven or eight riders coming hard behind them. The rustlers were using the horses as a living shield while also making themselves less visible targets in the dust and dirt being thrown up by the stampeding herd.

Caleb rose to one knee, and snapped off a quick shot at the lead rider, taking him off his horse and into the path of the following riders. Caleb's second shot caught the next rider in the shoulder as the man's horse jumped to the right to avoid the first outlaw Caleb had downed.

"Damn," muttered Caleb as he chambered another round and fired a killing shot through the wounded outlaw's chest.

Then the horses were on them, forcing Tip, Dos, and Caleb to duck low and hug the creek's bank as sharp hooves passed only inches above their heads. When the horses had passed Tip was the first one up and shooting, downing a rider only feet in front of him before he was grazed in the shoulder by a running horse and spun to the ground.

Dos and Caleb rose up as one and started firing at the five remaining rustlers. Dos emptied the Colt at two of the riders taking out both of them. Caleb, firing the Henry from his hip, snapped off four shots. Not having the time to take careful aim he missed with the first two shots but the other two found their mark. His target fell forward over the horse's neck and then out of the saddle, disappearing amidst the last wave of the stampeded horses.

Both of the remaining riders came out of the gap and veered to their left, taking them as far away from the gunfire as they could get. They were experienced riders and stayed low in the saddle and leaned to the left hoping that hiding behind the necks of their horses would offer as little target as possible. To Caleb it brought back memories of the fight in the Bella Vista canyon when the Comanche had used the same tactic.

Not liking what he had to do he waited for a break in the dust and horses blocking his view, looking to get a clean shot at the lead horse. A second or two later he fired one shot, believing he had scored a hit but not knowing for sure as once again the dust thrown up by the stampeding horses blocked his view.

Peering through eyes now beginning to fill with dust Caleb spotted the second rider just as he turned in his saddle and fired two shots. Taken at a distance of about 100 yards, and shooting from a running horse while looking over his shoulder, Caleb felt the outlaw's shots had no chance of finding their targets. What he didn't take into account was that good luck doesn't play favorites being as likely to favor the bad as the good.

The first bullet hit Dos in the upper part of his left leg, sending him stumbling backward, but fighting to stay on his feet he managed to get off two more shots before his wounded leg crumpled under him. The second of the outlaw's bullets struck a rock in the creek bed sending a chip of rock into the side of Caleb's head, hitting him just hard enough to throw off his aim as he fired a shot at the last of the rustlers. It was a miss but now Caleb took careful aim, sighting on the rustler's back, a target now more than 150 yards away, but a shot he was confident he could easily make. He took a moderately deep breath, held it for a second, and then slowly released it. Then he began to squeeze the trigger.

"Down!" he heard Tip shout from behind him, but before he could react or pull the trigger, he was sent hurtling through the air and face-first into the creek.

Dazed and barely aware one of the last horses from the stampeding herd had run over him, all Caleb could do was try to suck air back into lungs that had been emptied by the force of the collision. Sputtering from the water he inhaled instead, he turned his head so his mouth was sucking only air. He knew he was hurt but didn't know how badly. His left shoulder and hip felt smashed or at the least badly bruised and his eyes were blurry and slightly out of focus.

"What the hell…" he thought as he tried to force his mind back to the problem at hand. All he could tell was that he was wet, muddy, and unable to even get to his hands or knees.

Just as he started to try to fill his lungs with air and attempt to force his body upright, a strong hand lifted him under the arm and then turned him on his back. He felt water being splashed on his face followed by a hand gently tapping him on the chin.

"Caleb, Caleb…"

The words barely came through the fog enveloping Caleb's brain. His eyes began to clear as more water was splashed on his face and the tapping on his chin continued.

"Talk to me," he heard a voice command.

With an effort Caleb opened his eyes to see Tip's face staring down at him.

"Wha…?"

"You got hit by fifteen hundred pounds of running horseflesh, that's what," Tip told him. "You're lucky you're still in one piece."

Full realization of the events that had transpired only moments before suddenly came to Caleb's mind.

"Dos…he was hit, I saw him go down."

"He's okay, if you call being shot two times in one day okay. He's sitting up and looking at us so I thought I'd check on you first on the off chance you got yourself killed."

"The way I feel that may have been a distinct possibility" said Caleb.

For the next twenty minutes Tip did his best to patch up the uncomplaining Dos before catching the big gray Caleb had rode in on. All this was done with one hand and arm since his left shoulder seemed to be dislocated from the hit he'd taken during the first rush of the horses, or possibly from his turning Caleb over. Then, leaving Dos and Caleb with fully loaded pistols and making them as comfortable as possible, Tip clumsily climbed on the gray and rode for the ranch.

Before he was out of sight, Dos, with a slight smile on his face, said to Caleb, "Tell me, my gringo friend, is it like this everywhere you go?"

"No comprendo," replied Caleb in what he considered a fine Mexican accent.

Dos surprised Caleb with the only laugh he had ever heard coming from the usually somber gunman.

"What I mean to say, my gringo friend, is twice you have come to this place and each time you find trouble of the killing kind. First it was with the Comanche and now with rustlers."

"And twice I've ended up flat on my back, but at least this time I didn't get shot up."

"That was a misfortune left to me," said Dos, "but if I remember correctly, being nursed back to health by a beautiful woman can be a rewarding experience, no?"

"Yes," replied Caleb, "if you're talking about my wife."

"No, not Christine, whom I still love like a sister, but now I must confess my heart belongs to little Shannon."

Caleb thought back to the few seconds he'd seen Shannon before heading to the box canyon. She'd certainly done some changing in the past two years. Now taller and filled out, she had passed from a coltish girl to a woman of considerable good looks. Dos couldn't have made a prettier choice.

"Do I hear the sound of wedding bells in your future?" inquired Caleb.

"Perhaps, if she will have me," Dos replied wistfully.

"My guess is she'll have you and in the process make you an honest man in more ways than one."

"All I want in my life," said Dos as he reached into his vest pocket for cigarette makings, "is the love of a beautiful woman and a houseful of yellow-haired niñas and black-haired niños."

"That would be a good thing, and maybe the first niño will be called Tres. You know, as in Dos and Tres."

"Maybe so," replied Dos, "but tell me, why do you come here at this time? Is the reason just for a visit?"

"For Christine and my son, a well earned visit with family, but only partly so for me."

"You have other business in Texas?"

"Yes," replied Caleb. "As soon as possible I'll be heading for Galveston, maybe with a stopover in Austin.

"I would like to hear why you would be going to Galveston. I have many cousins there and you could say hello to them for me."

For the next ten minutes Caleb gave Dos a brief summary of the reasons for his and Christine's "visit."

"As I said before, I have cousins in Galveston" said Dos. "If you should need their help you need only mention my name. Although they are good family men and devout church goers like myself, they know much that goes on there, legal or illegal."

This cordial conversation, the first between these two men who had once come within a second or two of drawing guns against each other over their mutual affection for Christine, convinced Caleb the first people he'd look up in Galveston would be Dos' "cousins." This thought was interrupted by the sight and sound of an approaching buckboard followed closely by a man on horseback. Caleb recognized Shannon as the driver of the wagon but the rider was a stranger to him.

"Aa..ee..," said Dos, "the cavalry has arrived, and I think we could be in big trouble for letting me get shot."

Seemingly blind to Caleb's presence, Shannon brought the buckboard to a dirt-throwing stop only a few feet away from the injured men. Hurling herself from the wagon, she ran to Dos, tears already streaming down her face.

The stranger, a portly man of about fifty dismounted, but at a much slower pace than Shannon. It was as if looking at two men injured in a gun fight was an everyday occurrence to him.

"I'm Sheriff Croft and it appears as if you two fellas had a mite of excitement," he said as he stood, hands on hips, looking down at the fallen men. Only then did Caleb see the badge pinned to his coat.

96

"That we did, Sheriff," said Caleb with just the bare trace of a grin.

Without waiting to be asked, the Sheriff explained his presence.

"I just got back from my favorite fishin' hole when Rags found me. He told me about the rustlers hittin' Poke's place so I drug Doc Randolph along with me figurin' he might be needed if someone got careless enough to get himself shot. I got to the ranch house the same time Tip did, and after he told me about the scrap you fellas was in, I hightailed it out here to see if I could lend a hand. I tried my best to convince this here gal to stay behind, but she wasn't havin' none of it."

"Two of the rustlers got away," said Caleb.

"Just one," replied the Sheriff. "Me and the girl found one of them on the way here. He had a hole in his right leg with his other leg pinned under his dead horse. I can't tell for sure whether he bled out or broke his neck when his horse went down. Still, it's a shame it happened that way 'cause it looked like a good horse."

"The other rider," said Caleb, "big man on a blaze-faced black with one white foreleg."

"Me and Doc saw him in the distance just before we got to the ranch house. He was ridin' slow and easy, not breakin' any laws I know of, and since I didn't know about the shootin' I had to let him go about his business. Besides, if he's who I think he is, he's not a man I want to try to arrest unless I got more than a country doc backing me."

Dos, who was just managing to extricate himself from the arms Shannon had thrown around his neck, broke into the conversation.

"The Sheriff is a wise man, Caleb. I know well the man he speaks of and he is a killer. He is very dangerous and very good with a gun."

"His name is Roper, Jacob Roper," said the Sheriff to Caleb, "and he's got a bad reputation that stretches from Nogales to the Indian Territory. Until I saw him I thought the Rangers had either killed him or run him out of these parts."

"He doesn't sound like a man who should be running loose," commented Caleb.

"I'll try to get a posse up as soon as I can," said the Sheriff, "but it won't hurt my feelings none if after today he's long gone to parts unknown and out of my jurisdiction."

Once again Dos broke in, "Do not worry yourself about him," he told the two men, "I have a personal account to settle with him and as soon as I am healed. On my honor he will pay with his life."

"Sounds very personal," said Caleb.

"His raiding the rancho of my friends is something I have forbidden to those who make a living by night riding, so yes, it is a very personal thing. He knows the people here are precious to me and no bad thing should come to them."

Sheriff Croft, who had always harbored a respect for the sometimes outside-the-law Mexican, nodded in understanding and then shifted his gaze to Caleb.

"And you're Quinn," he said, "The gunman who rid this country of Toad and his band some time back."

"I don't count myself a gunman," responded Caleb, "but I am Quinn, and I did get in a little tussle with Toad…some time back."

"Thought so," said the Sheriff, "and on any other day I might have also recognized your Mexican friend, but not today and maybe not ever as long as he behaves."

He was speaking to Caleb but looking at Dos as he spoke. Before Caleb could answer, Dos, who had no trouble hearing the Sheriff's combination of warning and advice told Caleb, "See, mi amigo, I told you the Sheriff, he is a wise man."

Shannon chose that moment to end her silence.

"If you men are finished with your macho man talk, would you mind helping me get Dos into the buckboard before he bleeds to death?"

Given the sparks flying from her ice blue eyes as she spoke, both men knew her request was far more of an order than a question. Less than an hour later Dos was laid out on a bed and being examined by Doc Randolph…under the watchful eye of Shannon. After several minutes of poking and prodding by Doc Randolph the patient was declared to have "no life threatening injuries but the slug in his leg will have to come out immediately."

"You've also got at least two ribs that will need some time to mend and a chunk of missing shoulder that'll need some time to fill in."

"How long will Dos have to stay in bed?" asked a much relieved Shannon, who was now looking forward to nursing him for what she hoped would be an extended period of time.

Doc Randolph hadn't missed the loving look in Shannon's eyes and couldn't resist a little teasing at her expense.

"Well," he told her after giving a wink caught by everyone in the room except Shannon, "we'll start out by getting Dos into town where we'll…"

"I…you…he'll…," stammered Shannon.

Seeing the genuine hurt in her eyes Doc ended the teasing.

"Don't worry, young lady. I'll get the bullet removed in just a few minutes and then spend the night in case there are any complications. After that, someone with some skill at tending wounds will need to look after our patient for at least a week, if not more."

Hearing those words, Shannon's unhappy face was immediately changed to one of bountiful joy.

"Don't you worry, Doc," said Shannon as if she were taking an oath in church. "I'll look after him for as long as it takes."

She was talking to everyone in the room but her eyes were fixed on Dos.

Sheriff Croft, a confirmed bachelor who had little liking for either his own or hotel cooking quickly recognized that Doc's words offered an opportunity to enjoy a few sit down, female cooked meals.

"Someone'll need to go out in the morning to bring in the rustlers' bodies and round up their horses," he announced, "and how's I'm the Sheriff, I guess it's up to me. So if no one minds, Doc won't be the only one beddin' down here for the night."

After assuring the Sheriff he was more than welcome, Ann and Tip, with his arm in a makeshift sling to support his inured shoulder, approached Caleb.

"Now that Doc and the Sheriff are spending the night will you make it three?" asked Ann.

"It's certainly an appealing offer but I can't," replied Caleb. "Since the Doc has pronounced me free to travel, I need to get back to Christine and Sean Michael before she starts worrying about me."

Minutes later, after arranging to meet the Sheriff around noon the next day, Caleb left the ranch and headed for Liberty Hill.

Chapter 14
Surprises

The lone rider skirted to the east around the *Circle P*, sticking to the low ground whenever possible and using what cover the brush and mesquite afforded to stay unseen. He knew the men he had encountered in the canyon would not be able to pursue him, not with one horse between them, and therefore kept his black to an easy pace that wouldn't draw attention. Emerging out of a dry creek bed he was surprised to see two riders, only a few hundred yards away, moving at a gallop toward the *Circle P*.

"That looks like that Sheriff Croft and Doc Randolph," he told the black as he brought it to a halt.

Being seen by the two men would only be a minor problem because neither man was that handy with a gun, but still he hoped the sound of his voice would keep the black from letting out a whinny and alerting them to his presence.

After the riders had passed, Roper continued in a southerly direction, trying as he rode to work out in his mind the best route of escape from any pursuers. Familiar since a boy with running from the law, he dismissed any thoughts about going back to the camp site he had shared with his fellow rustlers. He could use the supplies back in the camp, but if one of his gang talked, the camp would be the first place the posse would look for him. It was the memory of the Sheriff heading for Poke's place that brought him to a decision.

"With the law out of town," he reasoned, "it would be safe enough to go into Liberty Hill, get a few supplies, and then see if I can't find out something about the stranger who pulled Dos' and Tip's fat out of the fire."

All the men who rode out with him that morning were either wounded or dead, a fact which caused him little concern or regret. They were easily replaceable by any of the numbers of outlaws that hid out in the Oklahoma badlands. What did anger him was the loss of the horses and cattle that would have brought at least a thousand dollars in Fort Worth or Waco.

He made a vow that if he could do so with little risk, somewhere down the line the stranger would be found and made to pay. And he had a good idea how to find him. Even as a hail of bullets were flying past him as he rode out of the canyon he was able to recognize the big gray the stranger had ridden in on. It was a horse he remembered seeing scarcely a month before, and the horse's owner was Rags Webber. What he barely admitted to himself was that it wasn't just losing the money, but possible damage to his reputation as an outlaw leader that was driving him to seek revenge.

"Time to pay a visit to Ol' Rags," he told himself.

Forcibly extracting information from a man was something Roper had done on several previous occasions. Doing it was something he neither enjoyed nor found repugnant. To him it was merely a means to an end. Once the information was extracted, a single bullet or a gun butt to a man's skull invariably ended the interrogation.

Shortly after his arrival in town, Roper left Webber's livery with the information he wanted. Not once did he suspect the lie that had passed through Rags' broken lips.

"Damn it to hell," Roper cursed under his breathe as he left the livery and headed to the town's only hotel. "Quinn! A farmer! He's nothing but a sod busting farmer from Georgia."

103

Five minutes later a menacing stare was all it took to get the hotel's room clerk to reveal a Mrs. Quinn and child had checked in shortly before noon and she expected her husband to join her that evening.

Confident of his skill and speed with a gun he decided not to disgrace himself by back-shooting a farmer, but rather to meet him face-to-face.

"Yeah," he thought, "I'll enjoy the look on his dumb mug when the first bullet slams into his gut."

****

Dark clouds and a chilling wind from the west caught up with Caleb during the last mile of his ride to Liberty Hill. A minute later he could hear a driving rain marching toward his back.

"Come on, boy," he urged the gray with a slight kick of his heels into the horse's side. "I know you're tired and so am I, but it won't do either of us any good to get soaking wet."

Horse and rider were only a minute away from the livery when a dense curtain of rain caught up with them. Now drenched and cold as they reached the livery, all Caleb wanted to do was get the gray fed and stabled, get a good meal for himself, take a long hot bath, and then spend the night sleeping next to Christine. The last thing he wanted was more trouble. It was the first thing that found him.

Reining the tired horse to a stop in front of the silent and darkened livery, Caleb swung from the saddle, careful as he did so to keep his right side close to the horse and out of sight. He had not been surprised to find the town's streets empty of people because the rain would have sent them indoors, but not seeing or hearing Rags as he approached the livery bothered him. It was nothing that would have worried most men, but years of living on the edge had taught him to be overly cautious when things around him departed even slightly from the expected.

"You done good," Caleb told the grey as he stepped out of the saddle. "I'll make sure Rags gives you a good rub down and all the grain you can eat."

"You won't be telling Rags anything," said a menacing voice from out of the dark and to Caleb's left.

Hearing the words, Caleb turned his head slightly to the left and saw a large man holding a revolver to the side of his leg, step out from around the corner of the building where he had been hiding in the shadows.

"And you won't be riding any more horses," added Roper, "unless there are horses in hell."

With his speech at an end, he raised his revolver.

The bullet entered the man's chest, grazed the heart, and shattered the shoulder blade. The man left standing then slipped his still smoking revolver into its holster as he walked over and looked down at the figure lying in the mud.

"Dos isn't the only person who takes it personal when his friends or family are attacked," Caleb told the dead man.

What Roper couldn't have imagined, and hadn't counted on, was that as "the farmer" swung out of the saddle he pulled out his Colt and was holding it next to his leg, out of sight, cocked and ready to fire.

The following day the buckboard carrying the sheriff and Doc Randolph rolled into town under a noon sun and came to a stop in front of *Bryson's Hotel and Saloon* where the Quinns were staying. Caleb, looking out of the window that faced the street, could see that the back of the buckboard was loaded down with an assortment of saddles, rifles, hats, holsters and even several pairs of boots. It was clear to Caleb the sheriff wasn't a man to miss out on a chance to make a little profit at the expense of dead men. Caleb then grabbed his hat and coat and with a "the sheriff's here" to his wife in the adjoining room headed downstairs and outside.

"Sorry I'm a little late getting here," the sheriff told Caleb, "but it took longer than I thought to bury that many men."

He didn't bother to mention that some of the delay was caused by his not finishing his second serving of Ann's breakfast until well after sun up.

"Not a problem," replied Caleb as he stepped off the hotel's porch, "but there's one more body over at Rags that'll need taking care of."

"You and Roper meet up?" asked Croft.

"If he was a big man riding a black, then the answer is yes," replied Caleb matter-of-factly.

"Just for the record, you care to tell me about it?"

"Not much to it. Roper worked over Rags with his gun butt and then waited for me. He had his gun, I had mine. Mine was better."

"And Rags?" asked Croft of the liveryman who had been his friend for over a decade.

"He spent the night in the hotel being cared for by my wife. My guess is right now he's being hand-fed lunch in bed, and aside from a slightly cracked skull and a busted up face, seems to be doing just fine."

"Speaking of the little man," said the sheriff as he switched his gaze from Caleb to the hotel's front door, "I do believe he's recovered enough to be out of bed and in the company of your beautiful wife and baby."

"To tell the truth," said Rags to the men, "Aah'm in better comp'ny than any of you reprobates would ever deserve, but in fittin' comp'ny fir a man like me…and Miz Quinn is as good a doctor as I ever seen, and by God that includes you there, Doc Randolph."

"I thank all of you for your compliments," said Christine as she gave the men a little curtsy, "but I would be even more appreciative if we could be on our way as soon as possible."

"Certainly," said Croft, "but before you go, I need to let Caleb know there are wanted posters out on five of the rustlers and if I figure right, it'll come to about fifteen hundred dollars."

Then turning to look at Caleb he added, "The reward money is yours to split up as you see fit, but it'll take a few weeks for me to get it from Austin."

"I don't want the money," replied Caleb, "but if Rags has no objection I'd like him to get five hundred of it. He earned it and most likely saved my life in the doing."

"Suits me," said Croft, "and the rest of the money?"

"I want Victor to get a hundred dollars and the rest goes to Shannon. She'll need it before long."

Twenty minutes later the buckboard, now empty of its cargo, was carrying Caleb, Christine, and Sean Michael toward the *Circle P*. Before they were out of sight, Christine could no longer contain her curiosity. With her right arm holding onto Sean Michael, she slipped the other under Caleb's right arm.

"Not that I object in any way," she told him as she rested her cheek against his shoulder, "but why is it that Shannon will need all that money?"

"Well," he replied," unlike yourself who came to our wedding day as poor as the proverbial church mouse, I felt it suitable that she should have at least a modest dowry."

"Dowry?" responded Christine, "You mean…"

"Yes, dear wife. The thing a proper young lady customarily brings to her marriage. It is an especially important thing for the bride to have if the groom happens to be of Mexican heritage."

"You mean…"

"You'll know what I mean when we get to the ranch and you have a chance to see how Shannon and Dos look at each other."

All a pleased Christine could add to the conversation was "Amazing."

Part 2

This nation will remain the land of the free only so long as it is the home of the brave.

~Elmer Davis

Chapter 15
New Orleans

"Let me see if I understand your plan correctly," said Phillip shortly before the ship was due to dock at the Front Street wharf. "I get the privilege of finding whatever backbreaking work I can on the docks, along with a chance to enjoy the comforts of a roach-ridden room in the slums of this fair city."

"You have a perfect understanding of the plan," replied Beau, barely able to suppress even half a smile, "and you need not thank me for affording you the opportunity to employ your full range of charm and muscle in a worthwhile endeavor, although I must admit to having more faith in the muscle than the charm."

"I appreciate your confidence in me, kind sir," replied Phillip with a matching degree of sarcasm, "and I'll be sure to remember it while you're suffering in the lap of luxury at the Bourbon Orleans Hotel."

As he spoke he also had to fight to keep a smile off his face. He knew Beau had mapped out their best course of action, but he still felt compelled to tease him about it.

"Sometimes a man is forced to do things that go against his sense of fairness," said Beau, "but I have good reason for suffering the indignity of staying at the finest hotel in the city while you are working on the docks and taking up residence in the black community. Almost everything that goes in or out of the city goes through the docks, and if there are any conspiracies going on in the way of counterfeiting, there is a reasonable chance someone working on the docks might know about it. You will be well positioned to see or hear anything out of the ordinary, anything that might hint at a conspiracy or the printing of counterfeit greenbacks. I, on the other hand, will have to glean what clues I can by rubbing elbows with the city's leaders and leading citizens. "

Beau had chosen the role Phillip would play in their search for the conspirators because as a black man, he could go where a white man could not and hear what would be said only to a black man. Beau also knew few secrets ever escaped the eyes and ears of blacks who worked as domestics in the homes and businesses of their white employers.

"I'd like to hear more about those indignities you'll be suffering," said Phillip.

Beau was ready with a response that was sure to further rankle his affable companion.

"Aside from one or two of the more elegant gambling establishments, the Bourbon Orleans is the number one watering hole for the most wealthy and influential members of New Orleans society. By staying there, I hope to casually reacquaint myself with some of my old Confederate friends who are part of that society. They know nothing of my role as a counter-spy during the war, and if some of them are part of the conspiracy, something I deem to be highly likely, they may see me as a good candidate for membership in their organization."

"So," said Phillip, "while I'm breaking my back on the docks and eating beans and rice, you'll be enjoying oysters on the half-shell and…"

"Don't forget the fine wines I'll be forced to endure," said Beau. "I may even have to force myself to eat a juicy…"

At that moment their conversation was brought to a stop by the arrival of a very tall and thin deckhand they had come to know as Elmo.

"Sirs," said Elmo in half a whisper, "we's about to dock and I's wanted to be sure Mr. Phillip here hadn't changed his minds about swappin' my old rags for his fine clothes."

"Not at all," answered Phillip, "besides, my clothes will look better on you than they do on me."

"Sho'nuff?" asked Elmo.

"You betcha'," said Phillip as he stood up to take his travel bags down from the overhang. "Besides, a deal's a deal."

Ten minutes later, now dressed in Elmo's clothes, he and Beau were looking down at Front and Canal Street, but from opposite ends of the ship. The war may have brought an end to slavery but the South still had long understood and established rules mandating a strict division between whites and blacks.

"Meet me at Jackson Square around nine o'clock and then we'll make plans to pay our respects to Lucinda," said Beau.

"After that we can meet every evening at the same time but at a different location."

Chapter 16
A Sublime Meeting

It was early afternoon when Phillip, carrying a suitcase filled with clothes and weapons, set out to find a room to rent. As far as Phillip was concerned the search for work on the docks could wait until the next day…or the next. Conspiracy or not he was in no hurry to start breaking his back working for ten to twelve hours a day. For now, all he wanted to do was spend some time walking around the city and getting to know it, starting with the area around and in the French Quarter. He also knew he needed to find a place offering room and board before darkness set in.

After an hour of slowly wandering the streets bordering the Quarter he was brought to a stop as he heard a melodious female voice coming from inside a small yellow and white house directly across the street from where he was walking. On the porch of the house was a sign advertising "Southern Food." A smaller sign under it read "Coloreds Only."

> *"I love you once*
> *I love you twice,*
> *I love you more than beans*
> *and rice."*

Phillip found her voice to be beautiful and the words intriguing, not just for their simple poetic quality but because they were the same words sung in the same way that he had heard as a young boy. He became even more intrigued when the source of the singing stepped through the door and stood on the porch.

She was tall, had long slightly wavy hair, and a full body hidden beneath a thin but well-made cotton dress that fell to her ankles. With her café au lait skin coloring, Phillip figured her to be either Mulatto or Creole. He would have bet on Creole.

Spotting him across the street, she placed one hand on a hip and asked in a voice that barely reached the awe-struck Phillip, "You are hungry, are you not?"

All Phillip could manage to do was nod his head at her.

"You have come to the right place for I can serve you a wonderful meal, but in order for me to do so you must first cross the street."

No other invitation was needed as a suddenly starving Phillip quickly crossed the café. As he was doing so the girl gave him a smile and then spun around and disappeared inside.

The meal, served at one of a dozen small unoccupied square tables in what once had been the front parlor of the house but now functioned as the restaurant's dining room, was more than Phillip could have imagined. Before him was placed a large bowl of steamed rice covered with onions, green and red peppers, black-eyed peas, bits of crab meat, all of it swimming in a thin brownish gravy that had a slight garlicky flavor and other spices he couldn't identify. After this came a side dish of yams covered in creamy butter and a cup of very strong chicory coffee that almost burnt away the roof of his mouth. Before he could even take his second sip of coffee a large plate of fried fish and okra was set before him.

After taking all the time he could to eat without being too obvious that he was enjoying her company as much the food, he asked her, "What do you call that first dish?"

"It's a local specialty called gumbo," she replied.

"It was as delicious a meal as I have ever had," said Phillip as he reached in his pant's pocket for money. "And now, what do I owe you for that fine meal and the excellent service?"

Her smile at the compliment was both beautiful and genuine, "As you say, it was delicious, so please pay only what you feel the food was worth."

"And who would I be paying for it?"

"My name is Adelia, and who will be paying me?"

"I'm Phillip and I thoroughly enjoyed both your cooking and your company, especially after spending the day moving bales of cotton from the docks to the ships."

It was a lie that had barely escaped his lips before he regretted saying it, but then again he wouldn't want her to think he was a rambler.

"Then a big hard working fella like you probably has room for dessert," she replied.

"Thank you but…"

"No buts," she replied as she turned away from him and with swaying hips entered the kitchen.

She soon returned carrying a cup of chilled custard and a small slice of cake drowned in a thick orange marmalade. By this time Phillip suspected more than one of Adelia's customers, entranced by her beauty, had paid considerably more than the price of a similar meal served in other restaurants. He also knew he would be no different.

"Adelia," he exclaimed, saying her name for the first time, "no glace du chocolat?"

"There was, but I gave it to the cat," she said sweetly.

Her words were followed by her walking behind him and ever so softly brushing her finger tips across his back. To Phillip her touch was far sweeter than the dessert. What he didn't know was the small touch told Adelia there were no apparent scars on the back of her new acquaintance.

After finishing the dessert and trying to inconspicuously wait for Adelia to return from the kitchen, Phillip reached in his pocket and withdrew a dollar coin which he placed on the table. Then, looking at the single coin, he changed his mind, added a second dollar to the first as he noisily pushed his chair back.

"Thank you, Phillip," he heard Adelia say from behind him. "If you're interested I also serve breakfast starting an hour after sun-up."

At her words he turned around and saw her leaning against the kitchen door frame, "I'll be here for breakfast bright and early," was his quick response as he got up from his seat and backed haltingly toward the door.

"Good," she replied as her green-colored eyes drilled into his, "Perhaps then I will learn who or what you really are."

The statement brought Phillip to an abrupt stop. "I told you…"

"You told me your name is Phillip and that may be true, but the rest of what you told me is something of a lie."

114

"Because…?"

"Because, my large friend, you claim to be a dock worker but your hands are soft and your nails have recently been trimmed. Also, because your not knowing what gumbo is marks you as a stranger to this city or any area within hundreds of miles. Then there's the matter of your clothing. They are threadbare as if they were all a poor black man could afford. They are also a size or two too small for someone as muscular as yourself, yet your generous payment for the meal I served you, along with the other money I saw you stuff back in your pocket, tells me you are capable of buying good clothes that would fit even such a body as yours."

"Anything else you care to share with me about myself?"

Adelia paused for a moment, and then slowly stepped around the table until she was facing him, making Phillip suddenly feel like a mouse about to be pounced on by a cat. Placing both hands on the chair opposite Phillip she gave him a long stare that forced his eyes to lock on hers.

"Your accent is both familiar and strange, as if you were brought up in the south but learned to form words after years of living in the north or east. You also hold your tableware and coffee cup in your fingertips, not with your hand clumsily wrapped around them. That alone marks you as a man of some refinement. You're carrying your belongings in a fairly decent leather portemonteau and not the burlap bag a common laborer would use."

"Your powers of…"

"There's more," she interrupted.

115

"If you want to impersonate a dock worker, you should at least wear a hat so that your well-trimmed hair, so unlike the real dock workers who sit at my tables, is not so obvious. My guess is you're also educated beyond the average person, black or white, borne out by the fact you know how to ask for chocolate ice in perfect French. So my deceitful friend, my guess is you're either running from the law, running from a wife, or perhaps you could even be a spy trying to steal my recipes. Regardless of who or what you really are, you have not been entirely truthful."

Phillip now stood silent, deciding what to do about this unexpected development, coming from such an unexpected source. He couldn't deny what she said because it was obvious she was too smart to believe any disclaimer on his part. He could simply leave without a word of reply and never return, but he knew doing that would be impossible because there was no doubt in his mind he was going to see more of this captivating young lady. Also, he reasoned, there was the slight possibility someone with her intelligence and knowledge of New Orleans could be useful in his and Beau's search for a counterfeiting operation.

"You have seen through me as if I'm a pane of glass," he admitted to her, "but I am neither a criminal nor a spy and there is no wife or family. As for your recipes dear Adelia, I would protect them to my last breath."

"Are all the men where you come from so outspoken and familiar, DEAR Phillip."

"…and are all cooks in New Orleans as eager to hurt their customer's feelings or do you just enjoy tormenting a poor soul such as me?" queried Phillip.

He was beginning to really enjoy their back and forth exchange, while at the same time hoping it might lead to something of a more romantic nature.

Her response was an almost musical giggle that slowly built up until it became a full throated laugh of sheer delight. When she was finally able to get her laughter under control, she stepped in front of him and reached up until both of her hands rested on his chest, a touch Phillip thought might burn clean through his light weight shirt.

"Dear sir," she began in an apologetic voice tinged with a touch of girlish laughter, "forgive my rudeness at your expense, but from the time I was a little girl, I have enjoyed analyzing interesting people, and you are a most interesting person. I study people's looks, how they speak, what they wear, anything that will give me an insight into who or what they are. It was a game I played as a child and have continued to do so since. I may have inherited the habit from my grandmother. It may mean nothing to a stranger to New Orleans but my surname is Laveau and I am one of the many grandchildren of Maria Laveau, the most renowned Voodoo practitioner and psychic in all of Louisiana, if not in the entire world. Fortunes could rise or fall depending on her predictions. My being related to her is not something I can prove because there are no birth records for someone of my blood, but I've always felt it to be true."

Phillip was more aware of the practice of Voodoo than Adelia could have suspected. He had spent some time in Jamaica on business before and during the war, and had been mildly exposed to this religious practice which came out of Africa when slaves were brought to the island to work the sugar cane fields. He respected the power the Voodoo queens and priests had over their followers but knew, like most religions he had come in contact with, it was built almost entirely on fear and superstition and ignorance.

117

When he looked at it from a more practical perspective, he felt Voodoo was nothing more than an elaborate con and as such no better or worse than other beliefs.

While Phillip was waiting for her explanation to end, he recalled the song she'd been singing, the song that caused him to stop on the sidewalk and listen.

"That song you were singing before I entered the restaurant…if I may ask, where did you learn it?"

"May I ask why you ask?"

"It's because my mother sang it to me at supper time. I haven't heard it since I was a little boy, before my family and I were separated."

"When I was young," she replied in a soft voice, "a lady who watched me while my mother worked sometimes sang it to me at dinner time."

Memories began to flood Phillip's mind, taking him back to the days spent with his parents at the Farrow plantation.

"What did she look like, this neighbor lady?"

"I don't really remember her face or her name. I was only about four or five when she moved away. I do remember she laughed a lot, was very nice, and made me feel like I had a real grandmother."

"Does anyone know her name or where she came from?"

"My mother would have known because they were good friends, but the yellow fever took her from me. All I have left of her now is this house that my father gave to her and she willed to me."

Suddenly Phillip could envision himself looking for this woman who might be his mother. A mother he hadn't seen since he was thirteen years old when she was sold separately from him at a slave auction in Opelousas. He knew looking for her was something he had felt the desire to do for years, but if he searched for her now, where would that leave him when it came to the search for the counterfeiters?

"Maybe," he thought as a plan came to him, "searching for my mother could be used as a good cover for the other search."

It was something to think about. Besides, no matter what he did at this point, he knew after meeting Adelia he wouldn't be tossing around any cotton bales.

"Before you leave, remember, I serve breakfast an hour after the sun comes up, every day but Sunday."

"I believe that will be quite acceptable as long as your food is served promptly upon my arrival. I wouldn't want to have to blame you for my being late to work on the docks."

As he had hoped, his light-hearted sarcasm brought out more laughter from her.

"One other thing before you go," said Adelia. "If by chance you haven't found a place to stay, Browns rooming house is on the other side of the block. Just tell them Adelia sent you and you'll get a better room than if you simply wandered in off the street."

"Thank you for that information…and you're right. I do need a place to stay, and the closer it is to a good place to find breakfast, all the better."

Five minutes later he was around the block and paying for two weeks lodging.

He was impatient to meet with Beau that evening and relate what he had found out about possibly finding his mother and to tell him about Adelia.

Chapter 17
Speculation and Possibilities

The lobby of the Bourbon Orleans was as Beau remembered it from the many times he had stayed there previously. It was spacious with high ceilings looking down on a floor of polished marble cut from the quarry in Pickens County, Georgia. Plush sofas and chairs were interspersed with ornately carved furniture by Francois Seignoret, the renowned French furniture maker who relocated to New Orleans in the 1830s and had a shop on Royal Street. One of the pieces was almost identical to a Seignoret sideboard Beau had in his Baltimore residence.

A dozen or so elegantly clad men and women sat about the lobby sipping either wine or champagne and seemingly waiting for the start of some gala affair. Their appearances reminded him of the need on his part to buy at least one new suit and several shirts to supplement what few clothes he had in his single travel bag.

"The old girl still looks pretty good," Beau thought as he crossed the lobby and stopped before the registration counter.

"May I help you, sir?" asked the prematurely balding young man behind the counter.

"My name is Rullman and I believe I have a reservation."

"Yes sir. We've been expecting you… and will you be staying long with us?"

"A few weeks, perhaps longer."

Paying in advance for two weeks' lodging and carrying a sealed envelope which had arrived at the hotel two days before, Beau found himself following a young man carrying his luggage up the wide curving stairs leading to his second floor suite. Half way up the stairway he stopped and then bent over and began touching his shoe. To anyone observing him it would have appeared he was having a problem with the shoe, when in fact it was done to allow him to look backwards under his extended arm to see if anyone was paying extra attention to him.

When entering the lobby, he'd noticed a large man in a corner chair with a copy of the *New Orleans Tribune* shielding his face from view. Now watching the lobby from the corner of his eye, he saw the man lower the newspaper and peer over the top of it at the stairway. A split second after he'd looked in Beau's direction he quickly returned to hiding his face behind the paper. Beau knew people are prone to looking at strangers, but the manner in which the man turned away indicated his was more than idle curiosity.

"Got you," he told himself as continued climbing the stairs, and then rounded the corner to the hallway leading to his room.

"Please take my bag to the suite," he said as he placed a silver coin in the bellman's palm.

Then, after counting off eight seconds, he returned to the top of the stairs and looked down over the lobby. A quick sweeping gaze told him the man with the newspaper had exited the building, more than likely through the front door.

"Foxes and hounds, and I'm the hound," thought Beau as he casually crossed through the lobby and out the front door.

His timing couldn't have been better. After taking three steps from the lobby, he was able to see his quarry step aboard a horse-driven trolley. The trolley bore the number 22. Hanging above the front window was a sign reading St. Charles Avenue. Beau watched from the sidewalk as the man from the lobby took a seat in the front of the car.

"Big man, rumpled brown suit and collarless white shirt," noted Beau, as he proceeded to commit the man's description to memory. "Light brown hair, maybe late thirties, and by the way he jumped on the moving trolley, good on his feet. It's a start."

With a degree of satisfaction he returned to the hotel lobby having already formulated a plan that would reveal the man's destination and identity.

Minutes latter he entered his room and opened the letter given to him by the registration clerk. A smile crossed his face as he read the terse note.

    B,

> *For the past week several men of questionable character have been canvassing the city asking about you. They told people to keep an eye out for you, and that a reward would go to anyone revealing your location. Be careful. You can find me at my place of employment.*
>
>   *L*

For the second time since meeting with the President, the leak that led him to believe he had been compromised, the leak he felt came from the White House, was confirmed. Two hours later, after having bathed and changed into fresh clothes, he was out of the hotel and looking for a good tailor.

****

After five days of calling on any person, store or warehouse Beau thought might be even remotely connected to counterfeiting, and meeting with no success, he found his way to Isaac Hinton's, the city's largest and best known printing shop. He had saved this call for last, reasoning that it was just "too obvious," a prime location to do some counterfeiting, and for that reason was the least likely to be involved in the conspiracy.

After identifying himself as a member of the Secret Service, Mr. Hinton, a small be-speckled man, eagerly ushered him into his office at the back of the shop. For the next few minutes Beau explained that he was looking for any information that might help him find someone capable of producing almost perfect counterfeit greenbacks.

"What you're describing is not work I'm capable of doing, Mr. Carroll. I am a printer and a printer only. The work you describe could only be done by an experienced master engraver, and they are few and far between."

"Do you know of any such man living in this area?" asked Beau.

"Not exactly," replied Hinton. "There is one person I can think of, a man who was once employed by the U.S. Bureau of Engraving and Printing. The problem is he disappeared about six months ago."

"Perhaps you would be good enough to tell me everything you can about this man."

As he made the request it was all he could do to hide the excitement of uncovering the first possible lead to the conterfeiting. Hinton's reply came immediately.

"His name is John Finley and he's without a doubt the most talented engraver this area of the country has ever produced. He's also a very fine printer and holds dozens of patents. As to the reason for his disappearance, I can't really say. However, the where may be Galveston. I know he used to talk about moving there and opening up his own printing shop."

Beau thanked Hinton for his time and information and had one foot out the door when Hinton made a last comment.

"By the way, Mr. Carroll, about a year ago other men, men whom by their looks I did not trust, were here asking for the same information as you just did. I told them nothing about John."

Beau left Hinton's shop elated that the speculation surrounding the counterfeit printer had been confirmed. Plans of leaving for Galveston soon filled his head, but before that could happen he had to make sure he had done all he could to uncover any counterfeiting plot in New Orleans. And then there was that problem with the man from the hotel.

He had a lot to discuss with Phillip when they met that evening.

Chapter 18
Scoundrels and Thieves

After discussing in detail the events of the past several days over hot chicory coffee and beignets, Phillip and Beau left the Café du Monde just as a cooling breeze came up from the Mississippi River levee that backed the coffee stand. The two men took their time as they strolled toward the Farmers Market seemingly enjoying the beautiful evening, all the while looking for any sign they were being followed or observed. Seeing none, they walked north for three blocks and turned left on Royal Street. A half hour later, after circling several blocks and twice back-tracking to again ensure they weren't being followed, they returned to Royal Street and minutes later stopped in front of the iron gate separating Ursuline Academy for Girls from its Chartres Street entrance. The meeting with Lucinda had been put off long enough.

As Phillip banged on the gate's clapper, Beau, knowing Lucinda's early history, thought it ironic that someone who was once expelled from a New Orleans finishing school after she had been arrested during one of her late night forays into the socially unacceptable and unladylike world of gambling, was now headmistress of the most renowned girls school in the city. Another remarkable fact about the academy was that it accepted white, black and Indian students alike. He was sure that fact, in itself, would appeal to Lucinda.

"It's so like her," he thought, "to defy the odds and public opinion."

Then, remembering her unmatched ability to read people, couldn't help but think, "I pity the poor girl who tries to get away with even a small lie."

Any further thoughts were interrupted by the appearance of a short, heavy-set colored woman attired in an overly starched gingham dress.

"I'm Hattie," she told them as she opened the door, 'and if you gentlemens are Mister Carroll and Mister Buckner, Miss Lucinda's been expectin' y'all."

After assuring her they were indeed the gentlemen in question, Beau and Phillip were escorted into the house and led to the parlor.

"You gentlemens make yourself comfortable," Hattie told them as she turned to leave, "Miss Lucinda will be with y'all shortly."

Beau couldn't help but notice that although her words were directed at both of them, her eyes were fixed on Phillip. She had barely left the room when Lucinda entered.

"Old friends" she said as she gave each of them a warm smile and a hug, "it's wonderful to see you again after all these years, but before we start complimenting each other on how kindly the years have treated us, let's discuss the primary issue at hand."

"Very well," replied Beau, while once again admiring Lucinda's lifelong and unfeminine penchant for never wasting time or words.

Beau opened the conversation by asking, "Have you learned anything significant about a major counterfeiting operation such as I mentioned in the telegram?"

"Quite the opposite," replied Lucinda, "nothing here would be of a particular interest to the Secret Service even though more than half of the paper money seemingly printed by the city of New Orleans is counterfeit. This threatens to put the city in a huge financial hole but doesn't have any national implications."

"However," she continued, "I have found the name of the man who has had people looking for you."

"Let me guess," replied Beau, "he once crewed on the *Sea Lady*."

"Not just a crewman," said Lucinda. "He was the captain and a survivor of the notorious Camp Douglas where he was imprisoned until the end of the war. He now runs several legitimate businesses but it is said his primary source of money is smuggling. He has a reputation for being ruthless, and, as I've been given to understand, those people unfortunate enough to have opposed or threatened his business in any way have a tendency to simply disappear."

Beau recognized the name Camp Douglas. It was a Union prisoner of war camp located in Chicago and well known for its cruelty and unnecessary deaths, indeed the systematic murder of as many as six thousand Confederate prisoners. Although Beau considered President Lincoln one of the noblest of men, a man of compassion and honor, he could never understand why Lincoln seemed to have turned a blind eye to the atrocities at Camp Douglas. How could the President, in his position of such great power, have failed to intervene, to put a stop to what the camp's commanders were having done to the Confederate prisoners? This was especially true when the camp was under the command of the degenerate and sadistic Colonel Sweet.

"Maybe he didn't know," Beau tried to tell himself, "maybe, as some rumors would have it, Secretary of War Stanton hid the reports from the President. It would have been like Stanton to keep word of the atrocities from the Lincoln's ears."

What Beau did know for a certainty was that men who survived such an ordeal were certain to harbor an unending hatred for their captors, the same undying hatred he had for any British authority. Never in his lifetime would he forgive or forget it was the British who had unjustly imprisoned him for over five years. And he could never forget that it was during those years his entire family lost first their home and then their lives.

"The man's name is?" asked Beau.

"It's Jack Drummond, or as most of New Orleans knows him, 'Captain Drum.' You should know that Captain Drum suffered the loss of an arm while he was a prisoner."

Beau then proceeded to relate to Lucinda all that had transpired since his meeting with President Johnson. He also told of his spying activity during the war which had led to the sinking of the *Sea Lady*, and of the information he received from Isaac Hinton that possibly confirmed the identity of the master engraver.

After listening to Beau's story, Lucinda remarked, "Isaac Hinton is a man of honor. Anything he shared with you can, you can take to the bank. And so, what's next?"

"Next," answered Beau as he glanced over at Phillip, "we sort out the problem with Captain Drum. Then, if there is nothing else to do here, we're off to Galveston on the trail of John Finley. Caleb should be making his way there also, so we can meet up with him and possibly make some headway regarding the counterfeiting."

Despite Beau's non-threatening words, knowing the two men as she did, Lucinda expected that blood would be spilled before the week was done. She also knew Beau and Phillip would most likely take the fight to Captain Drum before he took it to them.

The last thing Lucinda said as her guests were parting was, "Godspeed, and say hello to Caleb for me."

Chapter 19
An Unusual Ally

Two days later   Beau exited the hotel by a rear doorway and walked to the corner where Orleans crossed St. Charles. He had noted the same large man, in the crumpled brown suit, sitting in the lobby of the hotel on several other occasions. He decided now was the time to put into the action the plan he had formulated to learn more about the stalker.

An hour later he stepped aboard as trolley number 22 came to a stop before him. Taking a seat behind the driver Beau waited until the other two passengers had disembarked before talking to the driver, a slim man in his late thirties or early forties wearing a black suit and a cap that did little to hide his baldness.

"Sir," said Beau in little more than a whisper, "if you have the information I need, I have a five dollar gold piece I don't need."

"Did you say something about a ten dollar gold piece?" replied the driver without even bothering to turn his head to look at the man behind him.

He had done his looking when his passenger stepped aboard.

"Very well, my friend," said Beau, "ten dollars providing you have the information and that no mention of our conversation will ensue. In addition, I'll expect a return of my investment, if what you tell me is lacking in value."

Without speaking the driver reached an arm over his shoulder and extended an open palm toward Beau. Beau's response was to reach inside his coat pocket and remove a ten dollar gold piece which he placed in the driver's waiting palm.

"No problem, Mr. Carroll. You'll get your money's worth or my name isn't Jasper Lovoi."

For a moment Beau was speechless.

"How is it that you know my name?" he finally asked.

"Just a lucky guess." replied the trolley car driver with a shrug of his shoulders.

"It was more than that, Mr. Lovoi."

"Well," answered the driver as he turned his face to the right giving Beau a look at what was the man's half smile. "I been running this route for some time and learned early on it pays to keep these ol' eyes and ears open."

"A worthwhile endeavor if you don't learn something that could lead to ill health," Beau replied in a voice tinged with a threat.

"True," said Lovoi, "that is why I keep a loaded pistol where I can reach it. She packs a bit more punch than the peashooters some people carry hidden in their sleeves."

"Perhaps that's true, but let's talk about your knowing who I am," said Beau.

"Like I said, I keep my eyes and ears opened and the other day when Hatch jumped on my trolley before I stopped it, I naturally wondered if someone was after him. That's when I noticed you standing outside the hotel looking my way, or should I say Hatch's way, with more

132

than a casual look on your face. When Hatch continued survealing the Bourbon Orleans, I thought perhaps you weren't who he was after. But now, you've confirmed my first suspicions. Having to make a choice between dealing with you or Hatch, you're the easy choice. Although I don't know you, I do know Hatch and he's about as low a man as you'll ever come across."

"Tell me more," said Beau as he started to relax just a little.

"He has been riding my trolley for the past several weeks. Once he was in the company of another man and I heard them mention the name Carroll and how they needed to stop him. That's why when I saw your interest in Hatch, I figured you for maybe being Carroll. But when Hatch kept returning to the hotel, I thought I might be wrong. Then when you got on board just now, well, like I said, it was a lucky guess."

Lovoi spoke in a southern accent that Beau's practiced ear could tell was most likely manufactured.

"You mentioned a second man."

"Never saw him before or since but he was well dressed and left a twenty-five cent tip, and I never forget a big tipper."

"Could your lucky guessing extend to where Hatch gets off or where he might go once he does?" inquired Beau as he passed a second gold piece to the front.

"He puts off at Poydras, but I can't say where he goes from there. I do know, or at least the rumor is, he spends a lot of time at a dive just off Poydras called the *Treasure Cove*. It's not a place a gentleman like yourself would want to go unless he was backed up by a small army."

"I appreciate your advice and your concern for my welfare, but I believe I'll be putting off any visit to the *Treasure Cove* and Mr. Hatch until a later date."

"Just make sure he doesn't pay you a visit before that. I don't know about it personally but the word on the street is people who draw his eye tend to end up floating in the Big Muddy."

"Once again I thank you for your information and concern for my well-being. Now, if you please, I'd like to get off at the next stop."

Lovoi guided the horses to a stop on the side of the street as Beau stood up. A minute later, after handing Lovoi another ten dollar gold piece, Beau stepped off the trolley and was about to walk away when Lovoi's voice stopped him.

"One other thing, Mr.Carroll, the second fella, the one talking to Hatch, he had an empty left sleeve."

As the trolley pulled away it came to Beau's mind that he hadn't seen the last of this Jasper Lovoi. A half hour later, Beau met Phillip at their prearranged spot, a park just outside the Bourbon Orleans.

While the men discussed their plans for confronting Drum, they were unaware of the more than casual attention an artist seated at an easel not far from the bench was paying to them.

****

It was several hours past midnight the following night when the two rag pickers pushed their two-wheeled cart laden with an assortment of used clothes and shoes into the darkness of the narrow alley and came to a stop in front of the rear door of the *Treasure Cove Saloon.*

The larger of the two then reached into the pile of clothes and pulled out a long iron pry bar and jammed an end of it under the hinge attached to the upper part of the door. Ten seconds later the lower hinge gave way, followed momentarily by the upper hinge. Both men then stood perfectly still as they listened for any indication their breaking and entering scheme had been detected.

Once Lucinda had confirmed the saloon was one of Drummond's legitimate businesses, Beau felt it the most likely place to begin their search for any tie Drum might have to the would-be assassin sent to DC and to the counterfeiting plot.

After several minutes of silence, they shoved aside the door and made their way inside. Pausing only to light two small candles, Beau and Phillip moved past an array of neatly stacked whiskey kegs, passed through a set of swinging doors and entered the main part of the saloon. On the right was a long bar set in front of a mirrored wall. In front of the mirrors were dozens of whiskey bottles and drinking glasses. To their left was a carpeted staircase leading to the building's only other floor. Nowhere did they see any signs of a printing operation or any occupants.

"You look down here," whispered Beau, "I'm going upstairs."

"Ten minutes, no more," Phillip whispered in return.

That was all the time they felt could safely be given to securing information about Drum's whereabouts and his possible involvement with the counterfeiters.

Beau took the stairs two steps at a time until he was standing on the landing. He then turned right along the railing overlooking the saloon floor. To his left was a small door and directly in front of him, where the balcony ended, was a larger door. He chose the larger door thinking it more likely to lead to an office. He was right.

Standing in the doorway, the light from his candle barely reached across the large office. It was filled with furniture which would be more at home in a ship captain's cabin than in an office. A round topped seaman's chest sat in one corner with a ship's wheel hanging above it. To the right were a series of shelves holding books, rolled maps, a large cistern of tobacco, several ornately carved pipes, and a sextant. In the middle of the room was a six foot long teakwood desk with an opened ship's log on it. Behind the desk was a high backed leather chair which was facing away from the office door and toward the curtains covering a floor to ceiling window.

Beau had barely taken two steps into the room when the chair swiveled sharply around and he found himself facing a man seated in it. In the man's right hand was a Navy Colt. There was no left hand.

"Mr. Carroll," said the man who was only slightly illuminated by the candle held in Beau's hand, "It's nice to meet you at last."

Beau was about to throw down the candle and cast the room into darkness when he felt cold metal at the side of his neck. Now he knew not checking the smaller door was a serious mistake on his part.

"Raise your arms very slowly," said the man behind him.

At the same moment the man spoke, Beau could hear the crashing of glass and furniture coming from below.

"Phillip wasn't caught as easily as myself," thought Beau.

He then heard a thud followed by the sound of a large body or two striking the floor.

"I would advise you to do as you're told," said Drummond. "Hatch has no love for traitors or Federal agents and I wouldn't want any misfortune to befall you until we've had our little talk."

Drummond then left the chair, moved to a nearby lantern, lit it, and placed it on the desk.

"Mr. Hatch, would you be good enough to relieve our guest of any weapons? He looks unarmed but I doubt a man in his line of work would go anywhere without some type of protection."

Seconds later Beau had been searched and stripped of the two sleeve guns and a small dagger hidden in his boot.

"I see you're somewhat familiar with me," said Beau when the search was completed. "In that, you also have the advantage."

"One given to me by an artist friend, of late, and a distant friend prior to that," Drummond replied.

"The artist is unfamiliar to me," said Beau," but our mutual friend in the White House, Mr. Chandler, well, I'm afraid he will no longer be of service to you."

"Then that will be another debt you will pay dearly for," said Drummond as the muscles in his jaws tightened.

It was the first time a sign of anger crossed his face.

"And what would be the nature of these debts you feel I owe you?"

"Would you deny your part in the capture or destruction of blockade runners?" asked Drummond.

"I would not," said Beau, "but that was war and I was just doing my part, the same as you and your blockade running. It wasn't personal on my part."

"Not personal? You brought about the sinking of my ship and the loss of most of my crew, men I loved, men who had served with me for years. Even more unforgivable, one of the men who's death you brought about was my younger brother. You don't call that personal?"

"You have my heartfelt sympathy," Beau replied sincerely.

"Your sympathy is a poor exchange for what we went through. After our capture my brother and I were sent to Camp Douglas. No man should have to endure the suffering, the agony we were subjected to. It cost my brother his life and me my left arm…and you suggest sympathy is an acceptable exchange for that?"

In the light cast by the lantern, Beau could see Drummond's face, could see the anger starting to build to

138

the point of eruption. Beau realized at that moment that the infamous Captain Drum was irrevocably insane.

Before Beau could reply, from downstairs there suddenly came a frantic cry of, "Fire! Fire!" followed seconds later by an explosion which shook the entire building.

Beau could feel the floor shake just before a lead-loaded sap rendered him half unconscious. A minute later one of the men from downstairs entered the office. In a daze from the blow to his head, Beau could just barely understand the man's words.

"Captain, someone set a fire in the storeroom. We almost have it out but the big buck broke free. He jumped into the smoke and disappeared. We'd already cut 'im up some, and I think we got a bullet in him, but he's gone."

"See that the fire is handled. While you're doing that, we'll be taking our guest aboard the *Scorpion*."

Chapter 20
Narrow Escape

Forced to take one breath before he broke through the smoke and flames, Phillip emerged into the alley coughing and gasping for air, unmindful of the shallow burns to his arms and forehead. After blinking his eyes several times to clear out the smoke, he looked for the best avenue of escape.

Going back down the alley from the way he came would take him too near the front of the saloon. Turning to the left he had covered only a few yards when a sharp pain in his back caused him to stumble. Reaching back with his hand he felt a wet sticky liquid and then a hole the size of a walnut. It was then he realized he'd been shot as he raced through the flames.

"Keep moving," he told himself. "Drum's men won't need more than a few seconds to go out the saloon's front door, race around the back and trap my butt in the alley."

Ignoring the pain, Phillip ran until he reached the far end of the alley. He was about to turn right when a two-wheeled curricle pulled to a stop in front of him.

"Get in," said the driver.

Phillip couldn't see the man's face but it was a commanding voice, and "Besides," he told himself, "what other choice do I have?"

His weapons had been taken from him, his skull still hurt from where something hard had struck it, his back had a hole in it, blood was pouring from several cuts, and there didn't appear to be any suitable place to hide. Phillip dove into the carriage just as three men armed with pistols rounded the far corner. Shots rang out and bullets whizzed over the men in the carriage, but due in part to the darkness, and in a larger sense the shooters' poor aim, none of the bullets found their target. Having missed, all the frustrated shooters could do was watch helplessly as the curricle sped around the next corner and vanished.

"Sir," said Phillip, "I certainly appreciate the ride."

"You're welcome," came the reply, "but most of your gratitude should go to Captain Drummond because it's his carriage I borrowed."

"And you would be?"

"Jasper Lovoi, at your service."

"Beau spoke of his meeting with you but how is it you came to be here?"

"As you may have figured out, I'm with the Secret Service, and if you're wondering why I didn't reveal myself to your partner, please consider my position. Two weeks after my partner and I sent in our initial report regarding a conspiracy to manufacture federal greenbacks, he vanished. The only thing I could conclude was there had to be a traitor within the Secret Service. With this in mind you can understand why I was reluctant to trust anyone, including Beau. With little choice to do otherwise, I decided to continue the investigation by myself until I felt I could trust you."

"I would have done the same," said Phillip, "but how is it you happened to be at the *Treasure Cove* at this hour?"

"When I got off work last night I went to the Bourbon Orleans hoping for a 'chance' meeting with Beau. When I got there I notice Hatch hanging about outside the hotel. I was watching him, when you showed up and met with Beau in the park. After you left the park, Hatch went over and spoke to an artist who had set up shop near where you and Beau were conversing, then he took off in a big hurry forcing me to choose between talking with Beau or following Hatch. I chose Hatch and followed him back to the *Treasure Cove*, watched him go inside, and not long afterward he left.

I decided watching the *Treasure Cove* might be a better bet than following Hatch. So tonight, while doing just that, I saw Hatch go in and all the patrons, but him, leave. Then when I saw the lights go out and no one else left the building, it seemed kind of strange. I continued watching because I'd concluded the men inside were laying a trap for someone, and you and your friend Beau were the most likely candidates.

"Does that mean you're the one responsible for the explosion and the fire?" asked Phillip.

"Yeah, somewhat," came the reply. "When I saw that you had stepped into the trap I figured it wouldn't do anything but get us all killed if I charged in there with guns blazing, so I used some of the old clothes from your cart and a few gallons of good ol' one hundred percent southern shine to create a diversion. I intended to start the fire, but as for the explosion I can only guess somebody must have been adding a little gunpowder to the shine to give it a bit more taste. Apparently the gunpowder got left where the fire could find it. All things considered, I just wish both of you had been able to get away."

"Freeing Beau is something we have to do," said Phillip, "but if I'm going to be of any help in doing it, I first must get some medical attention."

"You're hurt?"

"Not that badly, but I've got a few knife cuts and some lead in me."

"Charity hospital is close by," said Lovoi, "but it would be a bad idea to go there because it's the first place Drum's men would look for you if they thought you were wounded enough to need medical attention."

Phillip knew the truth of Lovoi's words but he also knew he needed to get treated fast if he was going to be in any condition to help Beau.

"In the Faubourg Maringy on Frenchman Street there's a restaurant called the *Saint Jean's Café*," he told Lovoi. "It's run by a friend of mine and if you…"

"I know the place and I've heard about the girl who runs it," said Lovoi as he gave the sorrel gelding a flick of the buggy whip.

The light from the dawn sky had just begun to sweep across the city streets when the carriage pulled up in front of the *Saint Jean*. Adelia appeared at the door even before Jasper had helped a weakening Phillip climb down from his seat. A minute later, with Jasper and Adelia supporting him, he was led through the front room, past the kitchen and storeroom, and into a back bedroom where he was placed face down on a bed.

While Phillip remained silent, Jasper introduced himself to Adelia and then stepped out of the way as she began to tear away Phillip's bloody shirt. Seeing the wounds' severity, she was quick to act.

"Mr. Lovoi," she said without taking her eyes off Phillip, "I recognized the carriage you arrived in and don't think this is an opportune time to entertain the owner. I suggest you move it, preferably where it can't be found. While you're gone, I'll see what I can do about the scratches you're careless friend has picked up while he was out tomcatting."

Phillip wanted to laugh out loud, but with the pain from his wounds starting to grow with each passing moment, all he could manage was a muted chuckle, as he watched Jasper head for the street.

"I'll be back in an hour or so," Phillip heard him say as Adelia began using a wet cloth to wipe away the blood covering his back."

"Mr. Buckner," she said to her patient, "I'm not a doctor, but this isn't the first bullet hole I've treated, and by the looks of it I'll have to dig deep to get the bullet out. Then there's the matter of sewing up the cuts."

"I want you to…"

Before he could finish what he wanted to say, Adelia said in a soft voice, "What you want to do is keep quiet and stay still until I'm done. Its bad enough you've managed to scheme your way into my bed after we've only known each other for a few days, so don't compound your lecherous villainy by telling me what 'you want'."

And with that she left the room only to return seconds later with a clean cloth and a small bottle containing a clear liquid. She opened the bottle and poured some of the liquid on the cloth.

"What's that?" asked Phillip, wondering if he was about to be subjected to some Voodoo magic.

"It's something a Confederate doctor started using during the war. It's called chloroform and it's what I use on big babies when I don't want them cryin' or jumpin' around while I work on them."

"You're…"

Again Adelia cut off his words as she placed the chloroform-filled cloth over his face. He woke up more than an hour later to find Jasper and Adelia staring down at him.

"Well, the little man has finally started to wake up from his nap," said Adelia.

"Beau…he's…" Phillip could hear the words coming out of his mouth but they seemed so slow and slurred, as if he were drunk.

"I don't know," interrupted Jasper. "I've been back to the saloon, or what's left of it. Half the building is gone and there's no sign of Beau or anyone else.

Adelia took that moment to move between the two men, and start pushing Jasper out of the room.

"My patient needs some rest and by the looks of it so do you, so please, leave now."

Seconds later he was gone but not before he turned the sign on the door to read "Closed."

Part 3
An enemy generally says and believes what he wishes.

~Thomas Jefferson

Chapter 21
Ravaging Revenge

Beau continued to exist in two worlds, the nightmare world of London's Debtor's Prison which had held him for so terribly long and cost him the loss of his family, and the reality that after so many years of living with that memory he was once again imprisoned in a cold dark hell. He fought to stay awake, to understand where he was, but only after passing out several times was he able to regain full consciousness. Now he could feel rough boards under his back, boards that swayed slightly, boards that lifted him up and then down as if he were a lying on a living thing.

"I'm in the hold of a ship," he told himself. "And judging by the pounding she's taking, she's running hard into rough seas."

By the leaning of the ship to the starboard side he could also tell she was being pushed by a strong wind from the south southeast.

"We're sailing west, in deep water, and making about 7 knots," he judged. "Sailing west, heading for… western Louisiana, Texas, or even Mexico?"

Moving for the first time, he tried to bring his hands to his face to check the length of the stubble on it to give him some idea as to how long he'd been unconscious. Knowing this might tell him how long they'd been underway, and perhaps how far from New Orleans the ship had sailed. It was then he realized both hands were chained and manacled. A slight movement of his feet confirmed they were similarly bound.

"I'm spread-eagled, chained, cold, wet…but why alive?" he asked himself.

At that moment he felt a small body crawl up his side and move across his stomach. The animal's small feet scratched his skin as it scurried down his stomach and then to his leg. The scratching of the ship's rat on his skin told him he was naked. With that realization also came the knowledge that not only was he a prisoner, he was a prisoner of a madman.

Just as the rat scurried away, he heard footsteps overhead, the footsteps of several men followed by the sound of a hatch cover being lifted. The cover was removed but the hold remained dark, telling him that wherever the ship was, it was nighttime. A moment later four men made their way down the narrow and short flight of steps. The first man carried a ship's lantern, the second a metal bucket half filled with glowing coals, there appeared to be the handle of a fireplace poker sticking out of the bucket. The third man down seemed to be empty handed, and the fourth closed the hatch door after them. As they approached him Beau realized the third man down the ladder was Captain Drum. He closed his eyes, feigning sleep, hoping the men would then leave and give him more time to assess his situation.

"Mr. Colman," he heard Drum's say, "would you be good enough to wake our guest"

Seconds later the toe of Coleman's hard boot slammed into the side of Beau's face. Realizing the futility of any longer pretending to be unconscious, Beau opened his eyes, spit out a mouthful of blood and stared up at his captors.

"Good of you to awaken and join us," said Drum, "I was worried that the second time Hatch popped you with his sap, he might have hit you harder than I would have preferred."

"Your consideration and hospitality are something I'll long remember," replied Beau.

"As I remember the comforts of Camp Douglas," replied Drum in a voice devoid of any compassion.

He then reached behind him and took an unsheathed saber from the fourth man who had descended the ladder.

"This little jewel with its carbon steel thirty inch blade has been sharpened to perfection," intoned Drum as he waved the point of the blade only inches away from Beau's face. "It once belonged to one of the fine young officers in charge of Camp Douglas' prisoners. It's also the weapon which was used to remove my arm, so you might say that for me, it has both a personal and an historical significance. In a moment I think you will also have reason to remember it."

Beau remained unresponsive but watched as Hatch moved toward the timbers and gave the chain his left arm was attached to a hard jerk. Beau's arm was instantly and painfully pulled into a fully stretched out position as the manacles dug into his wrist.

"Very good, Mr. Hatch," said Drum, "and now, if you please, the tourniquet."

The fourth man then stepped over Beau's left arm, knelt down and wrapped a thin length of leather several times around Beau's upper left arm and tied it tight. Hatch then pressed his boot hard down on Beau's shoulder as Drum gripped the saber with his right hand and raised it high above his head.

"Now you'll feel what I felt when my arm was taken," he told his helpless victim, and swung the blade down in a long arch. The blade cut through muscle, then bone, then more muscle, until it finally was buried a half inch into the wood board under what had been a whole arm.

Beau watched as the lower part of his left arm, now severed between the elbow and the tourniquet, slid and rolled slightly away from his body as the ship rose and fell on the waves. The last thing Beau remembered before the darkness settled in was the sizzling sound of burning flesh as the hot poker was placed over the end of his arm.

Moments after the men left the hold, the ship's rats descended on the severed limb.

Chapter 22
Galveston Island

Two days after leaving Liberty Hill, Caleb was on the train that would take him the fifty miles that separated Houston from Galveston. The train was full and Caleb found himself sitting in the middle of and across from a family of four, a father, mother, and two teen-aged-looking daughters.

"If I may, sir," said the father addressing Caleb, "I am James McNulty, and this lovely lady on my left is my wife, Mary Elizabeth. Crowding your elbows are our daughters, Kerry and Danielle, both of whom seem to have forgotten their manners in their eagerness to peer out your window."

"It's a pleasure to meet you and your family," said Caleb, noting the man's copper-colored hair and heavy Irish accent. "My name is Caleb Quinn."

"Mr. Quinn is Irish like us," said the older of the two girls as she turned from looking out the window.

Her accent was an exact match to her father's and her blue eyes a match for the lakes of Killarney in the county of Ireland from which Caleb was sure her name was taken.

"Be polite, Kerry," said the mother with absolutely no conviction.

"Yes Kerry," piped in the younger daughter whose hair mirrored her father's, "but you know Momma's dying to find out if Mr. Quinn knows any of our relatives from the old country."

"Little lady, I have not been in Ireland since I was a about your age and sorry to say, as best I can recall, I don't know anyone named McNulty."

"What brings you to Galveston, Mr. Quinn?" asked James.

"Please, call me Caleb. I'm hoping to find some investment opportunities, and from what I understand, Galveston is brimming with the promise of golden opportunities for investors."

Again Danielle inserted herself into the conversation. "My teachers at Saint Francis told me Galveston is the biggest and richest city in Texas and has been first in Texas in lots of things. The first newspaper in Texas was the Galveston Daily News and Galveston, or Campeche, as it was called then, was the home of the famous pirate, Jean Lafitte. It was also the first city in Texas to have a medical school."

"As you may have guessed, Danielle is the historian in our family," said Mary Elizabeth, "and ever since we knew we'd be leaving New Jersey and moving to Galveston, she's been finding out all she can about the island."

"Daddy's a lawyer and is opening a big office there," said Kerry.

"It sounds like the beginning of a grand adventure for your whole family," replied Caleb, now beginning to thoroughly enjoy his conversation with this very nice family.

"It may be an adventure for the girls, but for me it's mostly about business," said the father. "If things go as we hope, I'll be opening a branch office of the company I work for, Purcell Exports and Imports. We feel that Galveston is the place to be if we want to expand our business into South and Central America, and most especially Mexico."

"It would seem that with all the political unrest, along with the ongoing tensions between our country and Mexico, you've set yourself a real challenge," said Caleb.

"All too true," said James, "which is why I have an appointment to meet with John C. Hill, a businessman, engineer and mining expert who has strong ties and connections in both Texas and Mexico."

"He sounds like a good person to know," said Caleb.

"As long as I'm passing myself off as a businessman," he thought, "I may as well seem interested in business."

"Are you familiar with the name John Hill?" asked Mary Elizabeth.

"Not at all," replied Caleb, "but I do know about Sam Houston, and Stephen Austin, and the Alamo."

"They are a big part of Texas history, and deserve to be, but I don't think any of them had the adventures John Hill experienced. The story of his life is absolutely fantastic," said Mary Elizabeth. "It all started in '42 when as a young boy of thirteen, he, his father and a brother joined the expedition to Meir."

"Mier?" asked Caleb.

"It was a little remembered argument over the ownership of a small town on the border. The Texans got an army together thinking they could scare off the Mexicans, but the Mexicans won the battle and took a couple of hundred prisoners, including John Hill his father and brother. John's brother and father were eventually set free, but only on the condition John allow himself to be adopted by President Santa Anna. It seems Santa Anna was so impressed by the boy's bravery under fire he wanted him for a son. John ended up living in Mexico and earned a degree in mining and engineering. He's now a successful businessman who lives in Mexico with his family but spends a good deal of time in Texas."

"Daddy says Mr. Hill has been a dinner guest of General Grant," blurted out Kerry.

"He sounds like a good man to know," replied Caleb.

"I hope so," said James, "because I'll be meeting with him the day after next in an attempt to put together a business agreement."

"Oh look," exclaimed Danielle.

The train was now only a few hundred yards from the long bridge connecting Galveston to the mainland. Already Caleb could the see the blue water of the bay and numerous fishing boats plying the water to either side of the bridge. Above the boats soared flocks of seagulls clamoring for their share of the catch. Moments later as the train made its way onto the causeway bridge Caleb and the McNulty family became totally absorbed by the view laid out before them. Large grayish birds with enormous and odd shaped bills were diving from great heights and crashing into the water. Sleek silver gray bodies of gigantic fish rolled above the surface near the fishing boats, and then disappeared beneath the bright blue water, only to resurface seconds later.

"It's the most beautiful sight I've ever seen," said Kerry.

Caleb had to agree. He had seen the dark waters of the Irish Sea and the blue-green Atlantic Ocean, but never anything quite so blue or filled with such an abundance of life. His trip across this same bridge on his first visit to Texas had been done at night, and did not afford him the opportunity to see the beauty unfolding before him.

"Then again," he thought, "my mind may have been on the promise I made to a dying enemy sniper, the promise that led to me meeting his daughter and the girl who became my wife."

As he continued to look out the train window, he ardently wished he was one of the dozens of people he could see holding fishing poles over the sides of the bridge. He was still picturing that and other scenes in his mind when the train came to a stop at the downtown 25th Street station.

"It was a pleasure meeting you," he told the McNultys as he reached up to take down his rifle case and travel bag from the overhead compartment.

It was seeing Caleb with the rifle case that triggered James' memory of where he had heard the name Caleb Quinn. During the war the *Philadelphia Inquirer* had run a feature story about the Union army's finest sharpshooter, a man whose exploits in battle had made him a legend. That man was Caleb Quinn.

"He certainly was a kind and gentle man," Mary Elizabeth told her husband as Caleb moved down the aisle in front of them.

"Not as gentle as you might think," mused James to himself.

Chapter 23
Local Aid

An hour later Caleb, had checked into the Tremont House Hotel, eaten a quick meal, and then made his way to the Texas and New Orleans Telegraph office. One telegram was waiting for him.

> SIR. PHILLIP WOUNDED BUT WILL RECOVER. BEAU MISSING. BELIEVED TO BE ABDUCTED BY CAPT DRUM OF THE SHIP SCORPION. BELIEVED SAILING TO GALVESTON THIS DATE. FIND PRINTER JOHN FINLEY. GOOD LUCK. TELEGRAPH ME WESTERN UNION.
>
> J LOVOI

The telegram had been sent two days before. Caleb calculated the *Scorpion*, if it was heading for Galveston, would take four or five days to reach port. That meant he had two or three days to prepare for its arrival.

"Time for me to call on Dos' cousins," he told himself.

It was a half hour later when Caleb entered the *Ship Ahoy Cantina*. It was still only an hour past noon and the place was empty of people except for an old man mopping the floor and the man behind the bar. Caleb made his way to the bar and ordered a beer. When he did the bartender gave him a long studied look.

"We don't get many gringos in here," he said as he reached for a glass, filled it from a tap, and then slid it over to Caleb, "so I think you must be here for something besides the beer, si?"

156

"My name is Caleb Quinn and I'm a friend of your cousin, Dos."

"I'm Tony Torres and I know of you," the bartender said as he extended an open hand toward Caleb. "Dos tells me many times of the rescue of the girls from the Comanche. He says you are 'the great killer' of the Comanche."

Over the next twenty minutes and a second beer, Caleb told Tony about his reason for coming to Galveston and the part Dos might play along the border. Then he recounted the most recent development as it concerned Beau. It was Tony who suggested their initial course of action.

"I regret to say I know nothing of anyone making counterfeit money, but starting tomorrow morning I will have people on the far eastern tip of the island day and night. The *Scorpion* is a ship they are familiar with and when she gets inside the channel we will know it. Once she's inside the channel it will take her at least an hour to reach the docks. That is plenty of time to find you so you can be there when she arrives. I will also pass the word someone will pay well to learn where John Finley is."

Then after serving Caleb a third glass of beer, he added, "money can do many things on this island."

"Thank you for that," said Caleb, "but there is one other thing. Are you familiar with a John C. Hill? As I've been told he's a Texan but lives in and does business from Mexico."

"Very much so," Tony replied. "He is well known as being a great friend to Texas where he was born, and to Mexico which he calls home. Strangely enough, even now,

157

if you wish to find him, he is a passenger on board the steamship *Gulf King* which is docked at the end of Bay Street."

Five minutes later, after leaving a generous gratuity and telling Tony he could be reached at the Tremont House, Caleb went looking for the *Gulf King*. As he walked through the Strand, he became more and more impressed with the city's obvious prosperity. Many of the multi-storied buildings were constructed of large blocks of granite that must have been quarried hundreds of miles away and brought to the island at great cost. The architecture of the buildings rivaled that of any city on the east coast. Elaborate bank fronts greeted their customers and the window displays in the clothing stores showed what he had to believe were the latest fashions from New York and even Paris. Apothecaries, furniture stores, cafes, jewelry stores, everything anyone could want to buy were in abundance. Street vendors crowded the sidewalks and corners. All of it reminded him of when he first arrived in Baltimore after leaving Ireland.

"Danielle was right about Galveston being rich," he thought.

He was also convinced it was the ideal city from which to print and distribute large shipments of counterfeit money.

Chapter 24
John C. Hill

Reaching the docks, he found them to be no less impressive than the business area. Ships by the dozens lay at berth with hundreds of sailors and dock workers loading and off loading practically everything the world had to offer.

"Caleb," he told himself as he looked at the flags of twenty or more countries flying from the yardarms, "you're a long way from Georgia."

Minutes later, he was on board the *Gulf King*, had introduced himself to the first officer, and requested an audience with John C. Hill.

"I'll see if he's available," he was told.

"When you do, please show him this," said Caleb as he handed over the letter of authority provided to him by President Johnson."

Five minutes later the officer returned accompanied by an eloquently dressed middle aged man.

"Please follow me, Señor," the man said with a slight nod of his head.

"Señor Hill is most anxious to meet with a man who carries such a strong letter of introduction. However, it would be most appreciated if you would leave any weapons you are carrying with the first officer."

Seconds later, the officer was left holding a shoulder holster and a belt knife.

Caleb's first impression of John Hill was that he was strikingly handsome and surprisingly young-looking for a man who had accomplished so much in his lifetime. He was dressed in a Mexican style suit which was lacking in the beautiful embroidery Caleb had seen on other suits worn by Mexicans of a high rank. He was, Caleb judged, not a man who needed anything but the strength of his character to make his presence felt.

"Tell me how I can be of service to you," he said to Caleb, "and please, call me John. I much prefer and enjoy the use of a single name while in this country as opposed to the four names I carry at home in Mexico."

"I am here on urgent business that possibly involves the welfare of both of our countries," said Caleb.

"I feel I am a true citizen of both countries," replied John, "so please continue."

Based on what Tony and James McNulty had told him, along with what he had observed so far, he knew the man sitting across from him was highly intelligent and experienced at dealing with problems at a high level. He was also a man, who would in all likelihood, instantly recognize a deception on his part. That he would be unsympathetic to the cause of the United States was a risk he felt he had to take if he was to secure Hill's assistance.

During the next half hour Caleb related to his host everything that had transpired since Beau's meeting with the President, leaving out only what had happened in Mineral Bluff and Liberty Hill. Not once during the telling was Caleb interrupted. When he was through talking, he waited for Hill's response.

"Mr. Quinn, should such a conspiracy as you've described even partially succeed it would, to say the least, alter the delicate bonds of peace linking Mexico and the United States, bonds I would do anything to preserve, if not strengthen."

Hearing Hill's words, Caleb was more and more convinced his trust in this man who lived in two worlds had been justified.

"Sir, I agree to the fullest which is why I risked coming to you. My associates and I, may with luck, uncover the conspiracy in this country, but there is nothing I can do south of the Rio Grand. I have a personal friend who will be making inquiries along the border, but he can't possibly accomplish as much as you, with your power and influence."

"I'm honored by the faith and trust you have shown me," Hill replied, "and when I return to Mexico, which will be in less than a week, I will call on every resource available to me to uncover any such conspiracy as you have mentioned. On that I give you my most solemn word."

"Thank you," said Caleb as he started to get to his feet, but was stopped by a waving of Hill's hand indicating he should remain seated.

"I must tell you that what you have told me reinforces suspicions of my own. It has already come to my attention through my contacts in the banking and mining world that a Frenchman using the name Jacques la Croix has been negotiating to buy very large amounts of gold and silver. This struck me as rather odd considering France's wars have left her virtually bankrupt."

161

"That is interesting," said Caleb, "and if it happened, it would mean that the conspirators could have in their possession enough gold and silver to resurrect at least some of the Confederacy. More than a few people in my country believe Jefferson Davis has been preaching such a resurrection since the end of the war."

"And on the other side of the coin" said Hill, "conspirators in Mexico would falsely believe they had enough cash to reclaim or buy back the western part of the United States. When it came out that the money was counterfeit, it could destroy the Mexican government and unleash another civil war on the people of Mexico."

"There is one major roadblock they must overcome if the conspirators even hope to succeed," said Caleb. "They must solve the problem of identical serial numbers on the greenbacks they try to use to buy the gold and silver. Unless they can solve that problem, all but a blind man would be able to tell the money was worthless, counterfeit."

"You are correct in what you say," replied Hill, "but I have to believe if any of my Mexican countrymen are willing to exchange gold and silver for greenbacks, then they must have been given assurances the problem with the serial numbers has been resolved, or will be by the time of the exchange."

For the second time Caleb rose to his feet and prepared to leave. And for the second time his host stopped him.

"One last question, if I may? How was it you became aware of me?"

"On the train to Galveston I met James McNulty, a businessman traveling with his family. I believe he has an appointment with you in two days. It was through him and his family that I learned of you."

"I believe I am now in that gentleman's debt," said Hill.

After disembarking the ship, Caleb went to the Western Union office and sent a telegram to Christine, followed by a second telegram to J. Lovoi.

Chapter 25
Renewed Friendship

The following morning, with nothing else to do and knowing the *Scorpion* wouldn't be arriving in port for at least two more days, Caleb took the Bay Street trolley to the beach where he spent several hours watching the waves gently lapping against the shore.

It was just as he was leaving that he saw a figure of a man he hadn't seen since the day he left the Farm to join the Union Army. The man was slowly walking just feet from the water's edge and looking down as if he were searching for shells. It took Caleb less than a minute to reach his old friend and mentor. He had approached him from behind, and was about to announce his presence, but before he could say anything the man suddenly spun around and reached under his vest.

"Jean Duvall, I'd say the last six years haven't slowed you down even a little bit," said Caleb.

For a moment the man continued to keep his hand on the revolver hidden under his vest, and then, as it dawned on him who was standing before him, his hand came down as he took the three steps separating them. Seconds later, they had exchanged a welcoming hug followed by Jean's customary check kisses, and then an American style handshake.

"I can't tell you how good it is to see you again," said Jean, "you look so much the same, but much more grown up than the boy who went off to war."

"Were it not for you and your teaching me how to use a revolver, the boy would not have lived long enough to become a man," replied Caleb.

"Then I will go to my grave knowing I accomplished one great good in my life."

"Tell me, what brings you to Galveston?" asked Caleb.

"Originally, I came here searching for fame and fortune, but finding neither, I decided to make my home here in the hope fame and fortune would find me," replied Jean. "Unfortunately, it has yet to happen. However, it seems to have brought us together once more, and that alone means I made a most fortuitous decision, but enough about me. You must tell me how you've been and what brings you here… but let's do it over lunch because I'm starving as only a Frenchman can starve."

Fifteen minutes later they were seated at the Island Sunrise Café.

"I would prefer you tell me what you've been doing these past years," said Caleb.

"If you insist, but I doubt it will be as nearly interesting a story as yours, being that you were a much publicized hero of the war," replied Jean, "but tell my story I will."

"When the *B and B* disbanded I was left with almost nothing except my talent for firearms and a nefarious military background. I considered returning to France, but suspected my being there would lead to an untimely demise. Therefore, I decided to go to Mexico and try to sell my services to Maximilian, which meant in some small way I would still be serving la France. In that I was successful, but unfortunately, after a long and deadly struggle the Juaristas took control of the country. Shortly afterwards Maximilian and his wife were executed. I myself escaped the same fate by only the slimmest of margins. After that, if I may say so, things got very interesting. During a month long stay in the Vera Cruz prison, courtesy of El Presidenté Benito, I became friends with a fellow prisoner and Frenchmen. He was quite feeble of mind, seemed to be an old man, and certainly no threat to anyone, but the Juaristas were imprisoning everyone with a French name and Dominique DuVreau was certainly French enough."

At this point, Jean was interrupted by a waitress who introduced herself as Jenny, and then took their order. When she left, Jean continued his story, pausing only long enough to cast an appreciative eye at the swaying hips of the departing waitress.

"During Dominique's lucid moments," he continued, "and there were very few of them, he had a story to tell that few men would at first believe, moi included...until he repeated it to me on his deathbed. I am not a believer in all that men say on their deathbed,...but a Frenchman?"

"You certainly know how to tell an interesting story," said Caleb, "even for a Frenchman."

"It gets even more interesting, mon ami."

"Dominique went on to say that when Jean Lafitte left Galveston in the spring of 1821, and Dominique was but twelve years old, he was a member of Lafitte's crew."

"As I've always heard it neither Lafitte nor any of his ships were ever heard from again, and presumably all of them went down in a storm, possibly even a hurricane," said Caleb.

"That is what history tells us," replied Jean, "but Dominique told it differently. According to him, after

166

Lafitte's ships sailed over the horizon and the navy ships that had been escorting them were no longer in sight, two of the ships continued sailing south toward the Caribbean, but the third ship carrying Lafitte turned west, and two days later dropped anchor in San Antonio Bay. The next morning, Lafitte and six hand picked men, including Dominique, took two small boats loaded with treasure north up the Guadalupe River, leaving behind Lafitte's mulatto woman and their son. He also left behind strict instructions that if he failed to return within thirty days they were to sail without him."

"So, Lafitte was a family man," said Caleb, as Christine and Sean Michael came to mind. The thought of them made him all the more anxious to finish the job in Galveston.

"I take it things went bad from then on?"

"Not at first, and in fact, just the opposite. Less than two miles up the river, they were met by four of their fellow pirates whom Lafitte had sent ahead several weeks before. They had with them horses for everyone and burros to carry the treasure."

"It sounds as if Lafitte had planned things out well in advance."

"Everything but where they were going to hide the treasure," said Jean.

"According to Dominique, Lafitte may have known, but no one else did. Anyway, they followed the Guadalupe north for six days when they encountered a lone Indian hunter whom they took captive. He was from no tribe they knew and spoke a language known to only one of Lafitte's men, along with a few words of Spanish. Counting on the

167

Indian's superstitious beliefs, he was told they were looking for a place to hide an evil god, somewhere so secret the evil god would never be found and freed. Two days later the Indian led them to a series of high hills, and finally to one hill that had a hole in the ground a grown man could barely crawl into. The Indian said it was a sacred place called The Land of the Dead, and had been called so for hundreds of years, since the time before the great beasts roamed the land. He told them tradition said the great beasts shook the earth so much that they made the big hole. He also told them the only way to find the cave was to know where the wild rice grows. The hole the Indian showed them led to a long winding cave that spiraled downward until it came to a series of underground pools of water, some of which were very deep. It was in one of those pools that Lafitte left his treasure."

Before Jean could continue he was interrupted by the waitress carrying their order. When she left Jean picked up the story where he had left it, noting as he did so that Caleb was so taken by the story to this point, he had yet to take a bite of food.

"So what happened after that?" asked Caleb.

"Lafitte and his men left there, leaving the Indian to act as an eternal guard over the treasure, and began backtracking along the route that had brought them there. It was on the second day out of the hills when their luck changed for the worst. They were attacked by a large number of Indians, probably from the same tribe as the hunter. The Indians had no firearms, only bows and arrows and spears, but over the next twenty-four hours were able to ambush and kill Lafitte's entire party, except for Dominique. Maybe it was due to him being so young, but for whatever the reason, his life was spared. He was kept as a slave to the Indians for more than ten years until he managed to escape and make his way across the border into Mexico. There he wandered the desert until he was found by a Mexican army patrol. By that time he was half crazy, starving and almost dead from thirst. They made him a prisoner in Monterrey for two, maybe three years, before they released him to spend the next thirty or more years as a street beggar. The rest of the story you already know."

"Except for what brought you to Galveston. Treasure hunting, maybe?"

"You are absolutely correct," Jean answered. "I had hoped to find someone willing to pay for an expedition to find the treasure in exchange for half of what was found. Much to my disappointment, all the big money people turned me down. I think they figured I was as crazy as poor old Dominique."

"They probably figured there are a lot of hills in that country and finding the right one would have been nearly impossible."

"True," replied Jean, "but there's one detail I left out as a form of insurance in case they wanted to mount their own search."

"You know what hill to look for?" asked Caleb, venturing a wild guess.

"In a way," replied Jean. "One of the last things that Dominique told me was that the top of the hill had the head of a sleeping man. I also neglected to tell them it is near where the wild rice grows."

"Then it really is a shame we didn't find each other sooner because I believe your story has a strong ring of truth to it, and I might have been able to find the money you needed."

"Thank you for that, my trusting friend," Jean replied, "but now it's your turn to tell me what you have been up to since the end of the war, and why are you here? I only hope your story is less time consuming than the one I subjected you to."

It took ten minutes to tell Jean all about Christine, their son, and their home back in Georgia. It took another fifteen minutes to tell him about the job he, Beau and Phillip had taken on. The last thing he told him was about the telegram he'd received from New Orleans. When he was done, he waited for Jean's response.

"Much the same as you when you arrived here from Ireland, Beau helped me when I came to this country from France. For that reason and several others, any trouble of his is also my trouble, and unless you tell me differently, when you meet with this Captain Drum I will be there with you. Even if I am not as young as I once was, I still have not forgotten how to point a gun barrel at something and pull the trigger."

"I knew I could depend on your backing me," replied Caleb.

The two men then agreed that starting at first light they would meet on the docks and wait together for the arrival of the *Scorpion*.

Chapter 26
Mans' Inhumanity

Beau was lost in time and pain, unable to judge how long he had been in the hold of the ship, aware only of the unending misery coursing through his body. The chains and shackles binding him to the ship's floor rendered him immobile except for the stump that had been his left arm. When he did slip into the painlessness of sleep, the ship's rats bit into the gangrenous wound until they got to the flesh that still had feeling. Their feeding on the arm would wake him up, but even then all he could do was wave the stump of his arm in a futile attempt to run them off. His being unable to move the rest of his body, combined with the dampness of the hold and the fever racking him, created a wave of leg cramps which caused his legs to pull up tight toward his stomach until they were prevented from going any higher by the shackles attached to his ankles. He suspected he was dying, and his only regret was that Drum wouldn't join him on the journey.

On what Beau thought was the third day at sea, he watched as the hatch was once more lifted and the four men again entered the hold and stood over him.

"I trust the accommodations are to your liking" said Drum, "I wouldn't want it said that I was a bad host."

Using almost every bit of the strength he had left, Beau replied, "You'll be dead before I am."

"And your death will come when I wish it," said Drum in a calm voice, "but before that time comes I want you to realize you have utterly failed in your attempt to prevent me from bringing down your precious country. As you may know, some people speculated that just before the war's end, Jeff Davis ordered the last of the gold in the

Confederate coffers be taken to Texas and hidden until it could be used to revive the south. Those people were grossly mistaken. There was never any gold, but there was something of far greater value, and I now have it. It's paper, and with it, I will destroy the trust people have in Federal money. I will also tell you that you are sharing this hold with enough of that paper, most of it left over from the Confederate printing operations in Richmond, to print millions of dollars worth of Federal notes. I assure you, in less than a month, I'll have more than enough nice new Federal notes to bankrupt the Federal government."

"Think what you like, you sick demented bastard," whispered Beau, "but you will fail, just as your precious Confederacy failed."

Drum bent over until his and Beau's faces were only inches apart. "I have heard enough dribble from your traitorous tongue," he said.

As he spoke, spit from his mouth sprayed onto Beau's face.

"After today your tongue will never again betray those who trusted you."

Drum then stepped away from Beau and toward the men standing behind him.

"Gentlemen," he told them, "now, if you please."

Seconds later rough hands forced Beau's mouth open and a block of wood was jammed between his jaws.

****

Caleb and Jean stayed close to the Tremont Hotel for the next three days, waiting and hoping for word from Tony that the *Scorpion* had been sighted. Their waiting ended when minutes after sunset, Tony entered the hotel.

"The *Scorpion* has entered the channel and should be dockside in less than hour," he informed them.

Minutes later the three men were sitting on the bow of a fishing boat tied to the 23rd Street pier. Twenty minutes later they watched as the *Scorpion* came out of the dark and slowly passed them before turning to the starboard. When she reached the Bay Street docks she slipped easily alongside one of the piers, and within minutes was made fast to the dock. It was a slick piece of seamanship even a non-sailor like Caleb had to admire.

In a voice slightly above a whisper Tony told them, "The man you saw standing on the bow, the one with one arm, he is Captain Drummond."

Caleb barely heard the words because he was already trying to formulate a plan that would get him on the ship without anyone on board knowing it. He did not want to confront Captain Drummond or his crew until he found Beau and affected his release. The thought did cross his mind that Beau might already have been killed at sea and tossed overboard.

"Why take him on board if all they intended to do was kill him," he reasoned. "Whatever the case, I've got to get on board."

"Tony" he asked, "I'm not that familiar with ocean going ships, so I'll ask you, how many crewmen would the *Scorpion* require?"

"Nine or ten, not counting the captain," Tony answered. "Maybe too many for two men to handle, but not so many for me and my cousins."

"The time may come when I will need the help of you and your cousins," said Caleb, "but for now I need to get on the Scorpion without raising a ruckus."

"Then I think we should wait until we see how many of the crew go ashore," said Jean. "My guess is they'll probably leave one, maybe two men on board after they unload their cargo, if they have any. The rest of them will head for Postoffice Street and the Red Light district."

Jean's words turned out to be somewhat prophetic. Less than an hour later eight or nine men came ashore and headed for the center of the town. Captain Drum was not among them, but several minutes later a buggy pulled up along side the *Scorpion* and Drum and one other man got in. It appeared that only one man had been left behind to stand watch over the ship.

"Caleb" said Jean, "I believe I should follow the buggy, and leave it to you to take care of matters on board the ship."

"I agree, but take Tony with you. Once you find out Drum's destination, he can come back here and tell me where to find you."

"And if you don't return?" questioned Jean.

"There's a contingent of army soldiers stationed near the customs building. Find them, and then do what you can to stop Drum from ever leaving the island. While you're at it, don't forget that Drum and his men are playing for high stakes and won't hesitate to kill anyone who gets in their way."

"I won't forget," Jean hollered out as he and Tony set off at a fast walk in pursuit of the buggy.

Now left alone, Caleb contemplated the various ways by which he might board the *Scorpion*. Walking boldly on board and asking for Captain Drummond was one way, but that could lead to a risky encounter with anyone who had been left behind. A second possibility was to use the darkness to his advantage and try to walk on board and hope he wasn't seen. A lantern burning just past the gangway negated that idea. The last choice that came to mind was to enter the water some distance away from the ship, swim to the ship's stern, and climb on board from there. He decided on the latter option, and minutes later, armed only with his knife, a wet Caleb squirmed over the stern side railing and set his feet on the *Scorpion*'s deck.

"So good so far," he told himself, as on hands and knees he crawled forward until he was crouched down behind the ship's wheel. It not only offered concealment, but also a bird's eye view of the ship's lower deck. He stayed there as five minutes passed, looking and listening for any sound that might help him locate anyone on board. Then, satisfied no one was topside but himself, he cautiously made his way to the deck.

"There has to be somebody on board," he told himself, "which means they're below deck, and that makes finding them and taking them out even more difficult....or does it?"

Moving quickly, Caleb left the bridge and made his way to the lantern, removed it from the barrel it was sitting on and carried it to the door leading to the crew's quarters.

He then smashed the lantern on the deck, just far enough from the door for the sound of the breaking glass to alert anyone below, but not so close as to prevent someone from climbing the steps leading to the deck. He could have used the fire to trap any crewmen below, but if Beau was on board, it might also have meant trapping him, and that he could not risk doing.

"Now," he thought, as he drew his knife and took up a position to the side of the doorway, "you can come to me."

Seconds later a single crewman scrambled up the stairs and through the door, almost walking into the fire started by the broken lantern. A second later Caleb was standing behind him with the blade of his knife at the man's throat.

"If you have a prisoner on board I want to know where he is or you are a dead man," he whispered into the crewman's ear.

"There's someone down below, in the forward hold," stammered the man.

A second later the back of the crewman's head was slammed into the doorframe, followed by his limp body being tossed down the stairs.

Caleb hastily squelched the fire on the deck by dousing it with a nearby bucket filled with water, and then moved quickly to the front of the ship.

****

Sometime earlier Hatch had entered the hold carrying a bucket filled with embers. In his other hand he carried the poker that had been used to cauterize Beau's severed arm.

He was a man who seldom smiled and seemed to take little pleasure in life, but now he was happy and had a smile on his face. When the captain was leaving the ship, he had given the prisoner to Hatch to "do with him whatever you like, but when you're done make sure he's dead and thrown to the crabs."

Hatch began by kicking his prey awake, and then informing him, "Thanks to you little man, I shared with the captain those months of misery spent at Camp Douglas, a misery I'll never forget. Now, after all this time, I get to pay you back by having a having a little fun."

Then he began.

Chapter 27
Sorrow and Revenge

Caleb moved silently toward the bow of the ship until he came to the open hatch. Then, after listening for a few moments and hearing nothing, he started down the stairs. Half-way down a faint light coming from his left and about twenty feet away revealed the backside of a bull-necked and rather large man who seemed to be poking a stick at something on the floor. Only when that something gave out a muffled groan did Caleb realize it was a man. Caleb instantly jumped down the last of the steps, feeling his foot land on a soft, furry body.

"Damn," he thought, as the rat let out a squeal.

At the sound, Hatch slowly turned his head in Caleb's direction.

"I told you"…his words were cut short as he realized the man at the foot of the steps was not the shipmate he expected, but someone unknown to him.

And it was as Hatch turned in his direction that Caleb could see it was not a stick the bull-necked man was holding, but a fireplace poker with a glowing hot tip. It was then the true horror of what was happening hit him…and that horror was surely being directed at what had to be Beau.

What Hatch saw was a man of his own height, but thirty or forty pounds lighter. With no shirt on, the whiteness of his skin stood out in the partial darkness. To Hatch's way of thinking the man was most likely a city dandy who had lived a soft and easy life…and was about to die for having the poor luck to be in the wrong place at the wrong time.

"This won't take long," he told himself, "and then I might have someone else to play with."

What he didn't see during the few seconds he took to study the figure at the bottom of the steps, was that the man had a knife cupped in his right hand with the knife's six inch blade hidden behind his wrist.

"I'm going to slice and dice you until you're crying like a baby," Hatch said to the man as he withdrew an Arkansas Toothpick from his belt. Then I'm going to have some real fun with you."

The two men inched toward each other, Hatch holding the hot poker in one hand and his knife in the other. By all appearances, Hatch could only conclude that the man in front of him was totally unarmed. When a bare ten feet separated them, Hatch was surprised to see his opponent suddenly throw his right hand out and point a finger at him.

"If he thinks pointing a finger…"

Before he could think another thought he realized he'd been struck in the stomach by something that hurt. Now frozen in place and bending slightly at the knees, Hatch dropped both of the weapons he was holding, and looked down at the front of his shirt where the handle of a knife was protruding from his stomach.

"How did that get there?" he asked himself as he slumped to his knees and then onto his back.

He had barely hit the floor when the man stood over him and pulled the knife free, causing Hatch to close his eyes against the pain. Instantly, a torrent of blood began to pour out of the wound.

"Press down hard with both hands and you might not bleed to death," he heard a voice say.

Hatch pressed down.

During the war Caleb had seen terribly mutilated bodies, both alive and dead, but nothing like the poor soul lying before him. Blood covered chains and manacles were attached to his legs and the one complete arm. Adding to the horror, Beau was covered in body waste and a bloody gag was tied over his mouth. Hatch had used the hot poker to burn out Beau's left eye, and part of the eye had fallen down and was stuck to the gag. Deep slices from a knife crisscrossed his chest and stomach, with the deepest of the cuts exposing a foot or more of intestine. He had to turn away from looking at what lay next to the intestine.

"Aaaah, Beau," Caleb cried out as his eyes began to fill with tears, "not you."

Beau stirred and partly opened his eye. This slight movement reminded Caleb that he needed to forget what he was seeing and concentrate on saving his friend's life.

With one hand, he gently lifted Beau's head a few inches off the floor. With the other hand he slipped the gag over the top of Beau's head and then pulled it away from his mouth. When the gag dropped away the horror of what he was seeing only got worse. Half of his friend's tongue had been cut off, and what remained had swelled up inside his mouth until it pushed out past his lips.

Caleb could hardly believe anybody could do what had been done to Beau, or that a man could live through such torture, but Beau's eye had moved, telling him that somehow, by some extraordinary feat of courage and will power, there was still a spark of life within that tortured body.

"I've got to get the chains off you before I can get you out of here," he said.

The reply he got back was an almost unperceivable shaking of Beau's head.

Ignoring Beau's gesture for the moment, Caleb moved back toward Hatch until he was kneeling next to him with the tip of his knife touching the man's cheek. Caleb was not surprised the man was still alive because the kind of wound he had, although usually lethal, often took a lot of time to run its course.

"The key," he told the man, his voice and the look in his eyes promising instant death if the location of the key wasn't revealed.

"Pocket," the man answered as he nodded his head down and to the right.

A minute later Beau was free of the chains and manacles that had bound him for so many days.

After tossing aside the chains and manacles, Caleb began to cast his eyes about the hold, searching for something to wrap Beau's naked body in before attempting to carry him off the ship. Tucked back where the two sides of the ship met and formed the bow, he could see what appeared to be a piece of sailcloth. He started to get to his feet to retrieve the cloth when a light touch of a finger on his arm stopped him. Beau had moved his one good arm until his hand reached Caleb.

"What is it Beau?" was all Caleb could say.

He then watched in silence as Beau slowly and painfully raised his hand, pointed it at his own head, and then curled his forefinger as someone would when pulling a trigger. The curling of the finger left no doubt in Caleb's mind what Beau was asking him to do. It was something no man should ever be asked, while at the same time, no true friend could ever refuse.

"I understand" said Caleb as he gripped Beau's trembling hand in his own. "I'll miss you, and I thank you for all you've done for me."

Then, after a moment of hesitation, Caleb slowly covered Beau's eyes with his left hand, while at the same time feeling Beau give his arm a farewell squeeze.

Seconds later Caleb's knife ended the life of Beau Carroll.

After wrapping Beau's body with a piece of the sailcloth, Caleb turned his attention to Hatch. Grabbing him by the hair and from underneath his chin, he pulled him within reach of the chains and locked a manacle to his leg. All the while he was doing this he was ignoring the man's pleas for mercy.

Minutes later, Caleb dumped half of the bucket of coals onto the stacks of paper the sailcloth had been covering. The other half of the coals he poured out of the bucket next to Hatch's head, but just out of his reach. He then carried Beau's body up the stairs, but not before looking back to make sure the hot coals were doing as he intended.

He never thought killing a man would bring him any degree of satisfaction, but it was a feeling he couldn't set aside when he saw the flames from the burning hold slowly making their way toward Hatch.

"If he has a soul," said Caleb to the night sky, "may it rot in hell forever."

Hatch never heard Caleb's words, but as Caleb stepped off the *Scorpion* with Beau's body in his arms, he could hear Hatch's screaming.

Chapter 28
Restitution

Caleb, once more armed with his Colt revolver, and carrying Beau's body, reached the beginning of the deserted pier and stopped. From the darkness to his right he could hear the footsteps of a man running toward him. Lowering Beau's body to the body ground, Caleb then drew the Colt and waited, braced for whoever the runner was. Seconds later a breathless Tony was standing in front of him.

"We followed them until they entered a warehouse on 31st Street, one block south of the Strand. Then, like you planned, I came back here while your friend stayed behind to watch."

Only then did Tony notice the rolled up sailcloth. The burning ship he had noticed when he was still a block away.

"If that is the friend you were looking for, I am sorry, but we will make them pay."

"Yes, what you see is my friend, and yes, they will pay, but for now I need you to take his body to the cantina while I join Jean. One other thing," said Caleb as he turned to go, "No one is to see his body…not ever."

"It will be as you say," replied Tony as he made the sign of the cross.

With a "Gracias" to Tony and a last look at Beau's body, Caleb turned away and started walking down the Strand. He wanted to run, to get as fast as possible to the warehouse, and to kill Drum, but running at night might draw attention, and that might delay what he had to do.

Several minutes of brisk walking along the right hand side of the street brought Caleb to the intersection of 31st and the Strand.

"One more block," he told himself as he turned to the south and began to walk more slowly.

It was at that moment that Jean, catching Caleb slightly by surprise, stepped out from behind a pile of empty crates.

"It's me," said Jean as a quick acting Caleb drew his Colt and dropped into a crouch.

"You're as fast as I remember, if not faster," said Jean.

Caleb didn't respond to the compliment. All of his thinking was concentrated on only one thing, finding and killing Drum. Nothing else mattered.

"Did you find Beau?" asked Jean.

"He's dead, murdered."

"Knowing Drum's reputation, I was afraid that might be the case," replied Jean, "but that means we have even more reason to personally deal with Drum."

"Tell me what we're up against," whispered Caleb.

Jean was quick to reply and answered like the former French officer he was.

"The H & S Cotton Company warehouse runs from 31st Street to 32nd, and takes up the entire block. Drum and the other man entered on the far end and haven't come out.

185

One man did come out, but because he was wearing a police uniform I felt letting him go was the smart thing to do. After that I took up position here because there is no concealment further down, and if the copper came back and saw me hanging around the warehouse, I didn't want to have to explain my being there to him."

"I guess Hill was right when he told me not to trust any of the authorities in Galveston," Caleb thought.

"Is there a way to get into the building without being noticed?" asked Caleb.

"I think so. There are doors on the far end where Drum entered the building, but if we try there we're liable to run into a guard or night watchman. I checked all the doors on the loading bays and they are shut and locked from the inside, so they are no good either. However, on this end is a row of windows used for ventilation. They are all locked but if we break the glass in a quiet way, getting in should not be a problem."

"Guards?" asked Caleb.

"None outside and no dogs," answered Jean. "There's no way of knowing how many people were already inside when we got here, but there were lights on, so somebody had to be home."

"Then I think it's time we paid Captain Drum a visit," said Caleb.

Ten minutes later they were in the warehouse and moving in the dark toward the far end. After moving past hundreds of bales of cotton, they found themselves looking across fifty feet or more of empty space separating them from a solid wooden wall built across the width of the

186

building. There were no windows in the wall, and only one door.

"They have got to be in there," said Jean, "but how do we get in unless it is with guns blazing?"

"Actually," answered Caleb, "I like the idea of guns blazing."

The surprise was total. Drummond and Coleman were hastily filling boxes with counterfeit money when the door was kicked in and two men stormed into the room. Caleb was first to enter with Jean a few steps behind him. Coleman, standing nearest to the door, went for his gun but was cut down before he could get off a shot. A stunned Drum made no movement at first, but after a second or two passed and the smoke from the Colts began to dissipate, he raised his arm and pointed at the two men standing in front of him.

"You," was all he was able to say before Jean put three bullets into his chest, all of them hitting him within inches of his heart and driving him backwards.

Caleb turned to look at Jean. The sudden killing of Drum, although well deserved, disappointed Caleb. He would have preferred keeping him alive, but only long enough to question him, to learn if there were any other conspirators. Caleb started to say something, but was forced to hold his words when a third man emerged from behind what had to be a printing press. He was not armed and had both hands held over his head.

"I believe your name is Finley," said Caleb as he noted the ink stained apron the man was wearing.

"Yes sir, I'm John Finley, and I'm not one of them. I was forced to work for these men."

"You have one minute to convince me you're telling the truth," said Caleb as he returned his revolver to its holster.

"He's telling the truth," said Jean.

As he spoke he continued to stand several feet behind and to the right of Caleb.

Caleb turned half-way around and found himself staring at the working end of Jean's revolver.

"Take off your gun belt, Caleb, and drop it to the floor," Jean told him, "and do it very slowly."

Suddenly things started to click together in Caleb's mind. The mysterious Frenchman mentioned by John Hill. Then accidentally meeting Jean on east beach. Jean's quick killing of an unarmed Drum after he pointed at them. Drum knew Jean. Jean is part of the conspiracy.

Had it been any other man Caleb would have gone for his gun, and given himself a decent chance of coming out alive, but not with someone as skilled a shot as was Jean.

"I suppose you've got a reason for holding a gun on me," said Caleb, as he unbuckled his gun belt, "and I think I know why, but I want **you** to tell me."

"I don't mind telling you my reasons," replied Jean. "Who knows, you might even understand why I did it."

188

Jean then lowered his revolver to his side and began walking slowly toward the table with the money on it.

"As I told you on the beach, I attempted to raise money to search for Lafitte's treasure, but was turned down by everyone I approached. However, one of the men who had rejected my request for money offered an alternative. Hitchinton made me a proposal that would pay me thousands of dollars. At the time I was out of money and nearly destitute. I had little hope of improving my situation. I was almost fifty years old with nothing to show for it but my skill with a gun. No family, no wife, no future, only the prospect of ending up with little more than Dominique. It was not the way I wanted to live out my life which made Hitchinton's offer all the easier to accept."

"Let me guess," said Caleb. "He wanted you to take the counterfeit money to Mexico and exchange it for gold and silver."

Caleb's words shook Jean on the inside, but on the outside he remained perfectly calm. Although his original plans were starting to unravel, he knew he could still end up with a large fortune, but he had to do it before the sound of the shots attracted unwanted company.

"That was Hitchinton's and Captain Drum's plan," said Jean, "but I had a simple plan of my own. It involved my keeping all the gold I got in Mexico, and to hell with them and their stupid dream of raising up the Confederacy."

"Jean, believe me," said Caleb, "whatever you do, there's no fortune to be made from this money. I've talked with John C. Hill, a name you should recognize, and he won't let you or anyone else trade paper greenbacks for gold or silver. All you'll get in Mexico is another prison cell."

"You're correct," replied Jean, "in that I do know who Hill is, but as for your telling me there's no fortune, you're sadly mistaken. There is over one hundred thousand dollars in this room, and that is fortune enough for me. I had hoped for considerably more than that but our clever Mr. Finley here has been rather lax in his printing efforts. Even if you have made it impossible to exchange the bills for gold bullion, I can still use them at their face value."

"Jean," pleaded Caleb, "forget the money and walk away from all this. You're too good a man to end up on the wrong side of the law, branded as a thief and murderer."

"I was once that man you remember from an earlier time, but not anymore, and it is too late to go back even if I wanted. Believe me, my last and perhaps only friend, if I had known you and Beau were working for the government, I would have done things differently. Instead, I find myself standing here, and much to my regret, pointing a gun at you."

"Do you intend to use it?" asked Caleb.

"Not if I can help it. Not if you give me your word that when I leave here you will not try to find me."

"I can't do that," said Caleb, "too much blood has been spilled."

"I truly hoped for a different answer," said Jean, "but your decision is what I expected from someone taught by people like Lucinda and Uriah, and if may say so, even moi. However, it's leaving me with no other recourse than to ask you to go for your gun."

"So you're going to give me a chance?"

"I owe you, and Beau, that much," replied Jean.

Caleb realized he stood no chance of drawing his revolver and getting off a shot before Jean, with his gun already in his hand, put a bullet into him. Still, he could die trying, and that beat the hell out off simply letting himself be killed.

"That is an unfair chance you offer my friend," said a voice from just outside the room. "But like you, I have a pistol in my hand, and I would be pleased if you would try to kill me."

Both Caleb and Jean turned their heads toward the door.

The man doing the speaking had an unmistakable Mexican accent and a voice Caleb easily recognized. Light from the room revealed the bottom half of a man standing a few feet back from the doorway. In his right hand was a gun shining in the light that escaped the room. The upper part of the figure was covered in shadow, but Caleb had no doubt about whom it was.

Jean, now faced with a decision similar to the one Caleb faced moments before, found himself at an equal disadvantage. Although he had his gun in his hand, he was facing with his left side to the doorway. In order to fire toward the doorway he would have to bring his gun across his body, an action which would cost him a few hundredths of a second before he could pull the trigger. He knew those fractions of a second could mean the difference between living or dying.

"I can do this," he told himself, "I will not be beaten by some would be gunman who thinks he is fast because he has been shooting holes into tin cans."

Jean made his move and it was fast, very fast. But there is fast, and there is bullet fast.

The bullet fired by Dos struck Jean high in the left shoulder, knocking him sideways, and causing his own bullet to go wide and bury itself in the doorframe. Dos' second shot entered Jean's head just below the ear. He was dead when he hit the floor. A moment later Dos moved out of the shadow and entered the room until he was standing over the body.

"He was fast," he told Caleb as their eyes met, "and I think maybe he was the one who taught you how to use a gun."

Yes," replied Caleb, "he was a teacher and a friend, and for most of his life, a man of honor."

"That explains why you are so good with a gun," replied Dos.

"That may be so," Caleb replied, "but it doesn't explain why someone who was shot to hell a week ago is here saving my life."

"Now and then I like to use my guns, just to keep the rust off them," said Dos, as a smile filled his face, "and I have learned wherever you go trouble of the shooting kind will follow. When the Baca family 'telegraph,' which goes far and fast, told me such an opportunity to use my guns could be found here, and seeing how Tip was tied up with the rancho and taking care of the women and your hijo and couldn't make it, I knew I was the last hope. So I did what any good Mexican would do, I came for the fight. "

Caleb knew Dos' explanation was far from the truth, and was being used to cover up Dos' real reason for being there. Despite the contentious nature of their initial meeting, these two men who had twice stood together to fight a common enemy, had formed an unspoken bond.

"Well, said Caleb, "as anyone could tell, I had everything under control. Still, I'm pleased you've recovered enough from your wounds that Shannon permitted you to come here for what you call 'shooting practice'."

"Perhaps my little Shannon was not so happy to see me go," replied Dos with a slight shrugging of his shoulders, "but that is tomorrow's worry, is it not?"

"Most certainly, and spoken like a man far from home," answered Caleb as he made a quick vow not to get between Dos and Shannon when they first got back to the ranch, "but before we discuss it any more, I need to have a few words with John Finley."

Chapter 29
The Scheme Revealed

Before Dos could reply the printer stepped in front of Caleb and held out his arms. On each of his wrists the skin was chaffed and red from what had to be rope burns.

"You asked for proof," he told Caleb. "Is this proof enough?"

"It's a very good start, but a little more explanation would still help."

"To start with," said Finley, "several months ago I was taken by force from my home and brought here, with the threat of a painful death if I didn't do as they wanted. Given their plans for the money, plans they made no effort to keep from me, I knew the minute the last of the money was printed I was as good as dead."

"That I certainly believe," replied Caleb, "but go on."

"I did whatever I could to slow down the printing of the money without arousing their suspicions. That wasn't too hard to do because they had no knowledge of printing, and even less know-how when it came to making the master plates."

"Did you solve the problem of printing the bills so that they don't have identical serial number?"

"Yes, but only to a degree. When I engraved the plates for the five and ten dollar bills I blanked out the area where the serial numbers should have been. Then I would make a run of thirty bills, all of them coming out with a blank space where the serial numbers should be. After that I would reinsert the sheet of printed bills and make a second run using a simple wheel of numbers that could be changed after each run."

"So," said Caleb, "you end up with thirty stacks of bills with no duplication of numbers within a stack, but duplicate stacks. As long as one stack was not compared to another, banks wouldn't know the difference…which tells me there were plans to distribute the money in thirty different locations."

"I'm impressed with your understanding of the solution to the problem," said Finley, "and glad it wasn't you monitoring my work."

"You claim to have done everything you could to slow down the process, but it seems to me you had things running very efficiently,' said Caleb.

"Well," said a grinning Finley, "I saved the best for last. When I made the second run to print the serial numbers all I had to do to mess things up was shift the sheets just ever so slightly off center. Then, when the bills came off the press the serial numbers would be slightly off, but enough so that it would be easy to tell they were counterfeit. This meant the sheets were worthless and the process had to start over again. By doing this I used up a lot of time while keeping the recovery rate for good bills to less than twenty-five percent."

"And in the process kept yourself alive that much longer," said Caleb, as he began to admire the ingenuity Finley displayed during his ordeal.

"It gets even better," said Finley, "it also used up a lot of paper, which is why Captain Drum had to bring more paper from New Orleans if he wanted to print ten dollar notes."

"I accept your explanation as you have stated it," said Caleb, "but that leaves us with the question of the engraved plates and the little wheel you devised. They'll need to be destroyed."

"Not a problem," said Finley.

He went to a nearby desk, opened a drawer, and removed a small box. Opening the box in front of Caleb, he then removed four engraved plates, two for the five dollar note and two for the ten dollar note. He also removed the wheel used to print the dates.

"I don't know how you intend to destroy them," said the printer, 'but I suggest you use a couple of well aimed bullets."

He then placed the engraved plates and the wheel on the floor next to Caleb's gun.

"May I," he asked as he placed a hand on the gun's barrel. "I'd like to be the one to destroy them."

Caleb hesitated for just a second, wondering if Finley's whole story might have been a very clever and well acted out lie.

"Go ahead," he told Finley, while shooting Dos a quick glance.

Dos, with his gun still in his hand, nodded his approval. A few seconds later Finley fired one bullet into each side of the molds, leaving them with a large indention where the bullets struck, indentions that would be impossible to repair.

"I believe my work here has now been completed," said Finley, as he handed the gun to Caleb, "unless there's something more?"

"There is one thing I'd like you to do before you're free to go. I want you and Dos to take the money you printed out back and burn it, but before you do that I'd like to know where you go from here."

"I'm not sure. I know I can't stay in Galveston. What's been done tonight has wrecked the ambitions of several of Galveston's more powerful and untouchable business leaders. If I stayed here they would make my life miserable, if not considerably shorter."

"I believe I know the solution to that problem," said Caleb. "There's a Mr. Hinton in New Orleans. He spoke highly of you and I'm sure he would jump at the chance to hire you if you asked…but even with that much distance separating the two cities, I do suggest you think about a name change."

"I understand," said John, as he moved to the table holding the money and began stuffing it into the bag Drum had been using.

When it and one other bag were full, with Dos carrying one bag and Finley the other, the two went out the broken door and headed for the rear of the warehouse. After they left Caleb took one look around and then made his way out of the building. He still had the body of Beau to attend to.

Caleb had taken only a few steps onto the Strand when a large group of men, some of them carrying clubs, barred his way. In the dim light he couldn't make out their features, but he could tell that several of the men in front were carrying axe handles.

Caleb, at first thinking they were members of Drum's crew, drew his Colt. Then one of the men to the front of the group spoke.

"You must be the Señor Quinn. My brother Tony told us to find you and our cousin Dos. I am Richi, Tony's brother. The men behind me are my cousins Rico, Jesse, Jose, Rudy, and little Dylan. He's the one with the light hair and skin."

"Yes," responded Caleb as he holstered his gun, "I am Quinn, and I'm glad to meet you, but I must tell you everything has been taken care of."

"We would have met sooner," said Richi, "but there was the small matter of convincing the crew of the *Scorpion* they would be better off if they returned to the pursuit of bad girls and good whiskey. Some of them needed more convincing than others, including a fat little policeman."

"Thank you for your help," said Caleb. "Perhaps later we can meet for drinks at your brother's cantina, but for now I need to attend to my friend."

"Meeting you later would be a good thing," said Richi, "sometimes a few glasses of tequila can ease one's sorrow, but until then I can only say, good luck and adios."

Chapter 30
Unsung Heroes

It was with an agony born more from his heart than the wounds that were still not healed after the run-in with Drum that Phillip re-read the telegram.

> BEAU DEAD. DRUMMOND DEAD. DUVALL DEAD. CONSPIRACY ENDED. FUNERAL IN 4 DAYS. GET HERE IF YOU CAN.
>
> CALEB

Thoughts swam in his head of all that Beau had been to him. Savior, teacher, supporter, mentor, friend, but most importantly of all the only "family" Phillip felt he had. The reality that Beau was no longer on this earth was a reality he was having a hard time accepting.

If not for Adelia, he thought he would simply walk down to the river and let the Big Muddy take him where it would.

Adelia...she became his anchor in this time of such abject sorrow. It was she who held him in her arms as he cried tears for the person who meant more to him than anyone in this world. It was she who listened as he recounted the story of his life with Beau. From slave to freeman of some renown. He knew that if Beau had not bought him from Captain Varvil those many years before, an action that occurred because of a chance meeting on the *Delta Queen* and Beau's recognition of Phillip's innate intelligence and goodness, that he, Phillip, would probably not be alive today.

Phillip knew he had to get to Galveston for the funeral and it was Adelia who agreed to go with him, not only for emotional support but also to continue nursing the wounds that for some reason refused to heal as quickly as they both wished they would.

They boarded the steamer at the Front Street dock and Phillip could barely believe it was only weeks before that he and Beau had exchanged their usual barbs with one another as they sailed into the city of New Orleans. Phillip and Adelia were accompanied by Lucinda and Captain Varvil.

The two had long been friends and were both almost as close to Beau as Phillip was. Beau had "rescued" Lucinda when she had no where to go after a scandalous incident aboard Captain Varvil's *Delta Queen* that ended with Lucinda being tried for, but acquitted of, murder.

The three day trip to Galveston proved to be a healing one for Phillip. Not only was he constantly consoled by Adelia but he was able to find a peace of sorts knowing that Beau had died for the country he so loved.

Using the trip as a time to recount the many escapades he and Beau shared served to embed the memories in a special place in his heart where Beau would forever remain the unsung hero of the United States.

By order of President Andrew Johnson, Beauregard Carroll was laid to rest with full military honors at the Galveston National Cemetery. The only people attending the burial, other than the military, were Phillip and Adelia, Lucinda and Captain Varvil, Caleb and Christine and Dos and Shannon. No mention of the funeral was made in the local paper. It was as Beau would have wanted.

Jean Duvall, at Caleb's insistence, rested in a grave in the fairly new Catholic Cemetery on Avenue K. His plot was bought by Caleb for his old friend and mentor. Caleb's belief was that Jean would not have really killed him, even if that was only a false hope.

Captain Drummond and his deceased crewmen were buried in the Cahill Cemetery adjacent to the Veteran's Hospital. The *Galveston Daily News* printed an obituary describing Captain Drummond as a hero of the Civil War and "The Last of the Confederates." It failed to mention that no one attended that funeral.

The obituary read:

*Captain Jack Drummond was laid
to rest yesterday at the Cahill Cemetery.
A veteran blockade runner of the
Civil War, Drummond helped the
Confederacy maintain much
needed supplies throughout the
war.
He was held as a prisoner of war at
the infamous Camp Douglas until the
war ended. He is considered the last of
the Confederate heroes residing in*

Galveston. He left no family.

An article in the *Galveston Daily News* recounted the tragic circumstances of Captain Drummond's death and that of several of his crewman aboard his ship the *Scorpion.* They deaths, it was reported, occurred in a fire that apparently started in the ship's forward hold. The men all died of smoke inhalation before the fire, considered an accident, could be doused.

The article was a testimony to what money can buy…

Chapter 32
Loose Ends

Caleb, Phillip and Lucinda sat huddled together on the Galveston beach.

They had spent the last two hours rehashing their history together and how Beau had managed to provide each of them a better life due to his generosity and kindness. It had been an emotional two hours of tears, laughter, and shared mourning for a friend who would be sorely missed.

As they got up to leave the beach and return to the others who would help them heal from their loss, Phillip was especially somber. He was at loose ends with no real place to go and nothing he was inclined to do. His entire adult life had been entwined with Beau, and now he would have to make a new beginning.

Adelia was waiting for him in the salon of the rooming house where they were staying. Going out to the large porch they found an empty settee and sat down while they discussed the future. Phillip was impressed with Galveston and especially with its treatment of black citizens. To his surprise he had discovered Galveston had several black political figures like George T. Ruby and Norris W. Cuney. There was even talk of establishing a public school system for black and white children.

Reconstruction was alive and well in the city, and Galveston was actually served by a black police force that had been appointed by the Union Infantry Commander, E. M. Gregory. Blacks from all over the country were making their way to Galveston because of the opportunities afforded to them. As he discussed the up and coming city with Adelia a more important idea began to surface.

"Adelia, I think we need to figure out where we're going to be living. Maybe here or maybe in New Orleans?"

"Did you just make a clumsy attempt to propose to me?" she asked, "because if you did I must graciously accept that proposal."

"You will?"

"Poor Phillip," said Adelia, as she leaned into his chest and took a deep breath, drawing in that rich man smell of his, enjoying every bit of it. "I've known since the day you stepped on my porch that we would spend the rest of our lives together. Call it Voodoo or whatever, but I KNEW. What I couldn't understand was why it took YOU so long to figure it out?"

Hearing her words brought an amazing feeling to Phillip. He now knew whatever life threw at him, he wouldn't be facing it alone. Life would be different without Beau in it, but it would go on.

Without any consideration for propriety he took Adelia in his arms and sealed their promise to each other with a passionate kiss.

****

Once back at the Tremont House, Caleb helped Christine pack their luggage. She was anxious to get back to the *Circle P* and Sean Michael whom she had left in Gram's care.

"Caleb, hurry, I don't want to take a chance we'll miss the train. I miss Sean Michael so much."

"I'm ready when you are."

Soon they were on board the same train, in almost the exact seats where Caleb had visited with the McNulty family. Dos and Shannon were seated two rows behind them.

"I met a very nice family on my way to Galveston last week," Caleb told Christine.

As he recounted the story of their conversations and how they helped him in meeting John C. Hill, Christine was barely listening. She was busy taking in the beauty of Galveston Bay that the train was now crossing.

Waiting until the train reached the mainland, Caleb then began a conversation he was reluctant to have.

"Christine, much as I want to go immediately to Liberty Hill with you, and much as I miss little Sean, I feel it is my duty to go to Washington DC and report to President Johnson all that has transpired. He needs to have all of the details, and I feel they must be given face-to-face in order for him to get the full meaning. Besides, some of the content should never be committed to paper, so even Jasper Lovoi doesn't know all the details. He was able to give the President a cursory report but I must fill in the gaps. When we reach Houston, I'll be changing trains for the east."

"Oh Caleb, I do understand, but we've missed you so much, and this short amount of time we've spent together will only make the separation that much worse."

"I know, but Dos will get you and Shannon safely back to the *Circle P,* and I promise I'll be there as quickly as I possibly can after meeting with the President."

Little did Caleb know when he set out for the nation's capital on the eastbound train Congress was in the process of bringing impeachment proceedings against President Johnson for violating the Tenure of Office Act because he'd dismissed Secretary of War Edwin M. Stanton.

The President's action was one Beau would have loudly applauded.

Chapter 33
The Wedding

Four months later, in mid March, a beaming Miss Shannon Edwards became Señora Emilio Baca, Jr. in San Antonio's San Francisco de la Espada Church, one of the missions founded by the Spanish in the 1700s.

On the groom's side of the church every pew was filled with Dos' friends and relatives. On the bride's side were Tip and Ann, Caleb, Christine and Sean Michael, a newly married Phillip and Adelia, Gram Szeliga, and Rags Webber.

The weather during the wedding ceremony had been unseasonably warm, but the dry cool night air that rolled in from the north made the evening perfect for the reception festivities which followed. The hundred or more guests, most of them Dos' relatives who came from as far away as Monterrey, were celebrating well into the night and seemed ready to keep going until morning. It wasn't a prospect that Caleb was looking forward to, but Christine had warned him that Mexican fiestas, especially a wedding celebration, usually lasted until the guests either collapsed from exhaustion or the liquor ran out. So far it was a good bet neither would happen until early morning.

Wanting to get away from the crowd for just a few minutes, Caleb led Christine to a wooden bench under a gigantic oak tree reputed to be five hundred years old. Tip and Ann soon found their way to the same spot.

"Isn't this the most perfect wedding ever," Christine said as she wrapped an arm around her husband's waist. "A magnificent church with beautiful grounds, lots of friends and relatives, and didn't Shannon look absolutely gorgeous?"

"This is only the second wedding I've had the honor to attend," Caleb replied, "but the first, although somewhat smaller, was by far the more perfect. As to Shannon looking beautiful, I certainly agree, but not quite as beautiful as another bride I knew."

"I can vouch for that," said Tip, "but we are probably talking about different brides."

"I was magnificent," chimed Ann, "but there is even more than the marriage we should be celebrating."

"What else could possibly be as important as Shannon's wedding?" asked her surprised sister.

"Well…maybe not for everyone, but certainly for Tip and me. We'll be welcoming a new arrival this summer. Sean Michael will finally have a cousin."

"Oh Ann, what wonderful news, why didn't you tell me before now?" demanded Christine.

"We didn't want to overshadow the wedding, so it just seemed right to wait."

As the sisters hugged and Tip and Caleb exchanged handshakes, the bride and groom strolled across the grounds and up to the group.

"Buenos noches," said a slightly tipsy Dos, "have my good friends grown too old to continue the dancing?"

Surprisingly, it was Christine who was the first to respond to Dos' humor.

"Unlike some young newlyweds who have yet to learn to save some of their energy for more important pursuits than dancing, old people like us know when to take a few minutes to rest."

"Aunt Christine," blurted out Shannon while also trying to hold back her laughter, "what if our guests heard you say something like that? They'd think Dos was marrying into a family of lecherous barbarians."

At that point Shannon could no longer contain her laughter and neither could anyone else.

"On that note, I think we'll call it a night," quipped Tip as he led a yawning Ann toward their room in one of the many haciendas that dotted the mission's property.

Good nights were exchanged and conversation resumed.

"Dos," said Caleb while still chuckling at Shannon's comment, "picking San Antonio for your wedding was a stroke of real inspiration."

"San Antonio," said Dos, "is the most beautiful city in all of Texas. It's also in the middle between Galveston and Monterrey, and not so far from the rancho, so everyone had about the same distance to travel. In addition, through my acquaintance with Padres of San Francisco de la Espada, I was able to secure the several haciendas on the mission's rancho grounds as a resting place for all who attended the wedding. That made it an easy choice. But now you must forgive me because the bride and her devoted husband need to get back to our guests."

Left alone, Christine was about to reward Caleb's flattery about beautiful brides with a less than lady-like kiss, but was prevented from doing so by the arrival of Phillip and Adelia.

209

"I'm glad we could be here because after this Adelia and I will be going back to New Orleans, and we probably won't see any of you for a long time," said Phillip after the couples greeted one another.

"New Orleans isn't that far from Georgia," said Christine, hoping Caleb would offer to take her to the city she'd never seen.

"That's true," replied Adelia, "but we won't be there for more than a month. Just long enough to finish looking for Phillip's mother, and for me to sell my café."

"And where to after that," inquired Caleb

"Baltimore," replied Phillip, "but only for the time it takes to sell everything I own and everything left to me in Beau's will. After that Adelia and I will make our home in Liberia."

"Not that I'm trying to change your mind," said Caleb, "but why Liberia?"

"We don't want to live where either we or our children are ever treated the way most black people are still treated in this country. We considered relocating to Galveston, but even such a cosmopolitan city as it, still has many problems between the races. Lincoln may have ended slavery but he didn't end the hate or the prejudice, not by a long shot."

"I can't argue that fact," replied Caleb, "but I do hope that some day we see you again, either here or maybe even in Africa."

As Phillip and Adelia walked away, Christine thoughts wandered from the new home they would be making in Liberia to the home that Dos and Shannon would be moving into when they got back to the ranch.

During the mild and slow winter weeks preceding the wedding Dos, Tip and Caleb had constructed a house, not far from the opening to the box canyon, that, except for its smaller size, replicated the one Joe Pokusa had built for his family. It snuggled up to the canyon wall, offered sunlit through windows large enough to use as rifle access but too small to allow man or beast entry, and had a strong door as further protection to its occupants. Dos had been the sole inhabitant of the house since it was completed.

When Dos, Shannon and Gram left for San Antonio a week before the others so that Shannon would have the opportunity to meet her soon to be in-laws prior to the wedding itself, Ann and Christine had commandeered the refurbishing of the house. They cleaned it from ceiling to floor ridding it of all the dirt accumulated by its bachelor resident. Then Ann, using her natural flair for decorating and her sister's help, transformed the house into a home. It now was not only sparkling clean but held an assortment of furnishings that made it cozy and comfortable. In addition to dried flowers placed in vases or tied with ribbons and scattered about in nooks and crannies, there were scoured pots and pans the women had found in the rafters of the barn, an assortment of dishes and cutlery on the kitchen's baker rack, a beautiful hand-made quilt purchased by Tip and Ann on a recent trip to Wimberly adorned the bed, needlepoint pillows and tatted doilies graced the furniture, and a painting of the fields of Poland covered in wildflowers graced the wall above the fireplace mantel. Gram had contributed the painting so that, as she put it, "Shannon would have the wildflowers she so loved in her home every day."

Ann and Christine had coerced Tip and Caleb into building benches for the front porch, and a gun case for the rifles they removed from the wall where they hung Gram's painting.

Christine couldn't wait to see the look on the faces of the newlyweds when they returned to their home.

Meanwhile, Caleb tried to get his mind off Phillip's words by bringing the conversation with Christine back to Shannon and the wedding.

"As great as this wedding is, I hope Shannon saved some of her dowry for later, because from what I've heard around the old wine barrel, she and Dos paid for everyone's transportation, along with room and board."

"I hear things too," Christine said, "and I know for a fact our frugal little Shannon still has all of her dowry except for what was spent on her wedding dress."

"Then how the heck did they have enough money to pay for transportation, hacienda rooms, the church, two Mariachi bands, and all that food and drink?"

"As I understand it, from what I heard around the old punch bowl, a handful or two of the counterfeit money from the warehouse simply would not burn, no matter how hard Dos and the Finley gentleman tried. Even some of Dos' cousins tried to burn the money and failed."

"Those scoundrels," said a laughing Caleb with a shake of his head.

"So, my dear husband, you're not angry?"

"How could I be angry? All of them, Dos and his cousins, and even John Finley, earned every single greenback they could stuff in their pockets…not to mention what I owe them for saving my life, or what the government owes them for preventing a national calamity."

"Now that that's settled," said Christine, "there's another small matter we need to talk about."

"Are you pregnant, too?"

"No I'm not, but we can work on that later. However, what I want to know does concern us."

"Fire away," said a bemused Caleb.

"Well," said Christine as she gave him her most engaging smile, "we already know that when Tip and Dos get back to the ranch they plan to hire on a dozen hands to round up as many wild cattle as they can before spring gets here. Then they're going to take them to Fort Sumner, New Mexico by following the newly blazed Goodnight-Loving Trail. We now also know what Phillip and Adelia have planned. What I don't know is what we'll be doing in the three weeks we have left here before we need to get back home and start the planting."

"You, my dear, can spend those three weeks comforting your sister and Shannon and preparing them for what life will be like when their unworthy and callous husbands head for Kansas."

"And what will my unworthy and callous husband be doing while I'm doing all that comforting?"

"I think I'll go searching the hills for a man sleeping near a hole in the ground surrounded by wild rice."

A moment or two later, a smiling Christine remembered the reward she wanted to give her very special husband. Somewhere in the middle of the kiss that followed she decided that Ann and Shannon would have to get by with comforting each other.

Novel Facts

President James Madison's escape from the White House in 1814 when it was attacked by British soldiers is a true event. His wife, Dolly, is credited with saving several national treasures from destruction by taking some with her when the family escaped and shipping some out of the city before the attack.

The **Hotel Monaco** is a Washington D.C. hotel that occupies what was the general post office for the city built in 1839. In 1845 the first public telegraph in the United States was opened in the building by Samuel Morse. The building was eventually converted into a hotel which the author conveniently decided to use through poetic license as being opened after the Civil War rather than in 2002.

President Andrew Johnson was the 17th president of the United States. He took office upon the assassination of Abraham Lincoln. It fell on his shoulders to enact the Reconstruction of the southern states when the nation reunited after the Civil War.

The Secret Service

The **Pinkerton Agency** was opened by **Allen Pinkerton** in the 1850s. During the Civil War Pinkerton served as the head of the Union Intelligence Service. He stopped an assassination plot while guarding President Lincoln and his agents often worked undercover posing as Confederate soldiers. The Union Intelligence Service was a forerunner of the Secret Service.

In 1865, the **United States Secret Service** was established as a part of the Bureau of the Treasury. It was created for the purpose of controlling counterfeiters who were destroying the faith of the public in the nation's currency.

The **secret tunnel under the White House** described in the book is a fabrication of the author's imagination, however there does exist an extensive secret underground tunnel system that links the White House to various government buildings throughout Washington DC and that includes the Emergency Operations Center, a subterranean bunker located under the East Wing of the White House.

Berdan's snipers were men of the 1st and 2nd Regiments of the United States Sharp Shooters commanded by Hiram Berdan during the Civil War.

A **Presidential Order of Authority** is an executive order, not authorized by Congress. Its basis for justification is that the power is inherently granted to the Executive by the Constitution.

James Rood Doolittle was a United States senator from Wisconsin who served in that capacity from 1854 – 1869. He was a strong supporter of President Andrew Johnson.

The **Trail of Those Who Cried** is the Cherokee name for the **Trail of Tears**, a forced march of 15,000 Cherokee Indians from their lands east of the Mississippi River to Indian Territory in what is now present day Oklahoma. The march was part of Andrew Jackson's Indian Removal policy. Over 4,000 of the Cherokee died during the march due to hunger, exhaustion and disease.

Fort Butler in what is now Murphy, North Carolina was used as the main collection point for the Cherokee people on the eastern side of the mountains.

The Company of Copper Hill Copper Mine located in Copper Hill, Tennessee was the site of one of many metal mining operations that arose in the Copper Basin area. Copper was discovered in the area in 1820 and speculators quickly invested in mining production using the local mountain people to do the brunt of the work.

The **Ku Klux Klan (KKK)** was formed by Confederate Army veterans in 1865. The first social club, as the Klan was called, developed in Pulaski, Tennessee. At a convention in Nashville, Tennessee in 1867 the KKK became the "Invisible Empire of the South." The first Grand Wizard is believed to have been General Nathan Bedford Forrest. The group became a terrorist-type organization during Reconstruction, hoping to destroy it by murdering blacks and whites who were active in Radical Reconstruction politics or were helping to educate blacks. The Klan also targeted churches, especially those with black populations and Catholics. The Klansmen wore hooded robes to hide their identities, burned crosses on people's and institutions' lawns, and participated in lynchings. They were often called night riders.

The **impeachment of Andrew Johnson** was sought by Radical Republicans in Congress. In 1867, the Radical Republicans who controlled the United States Congress placed the southern states under military rule as a means of affecting their own plans for reconstruction of the south. Congress passed laws that placed restrictions on Johnson, as President of the United Stated. Congress alleged that Johnson violated the Tenure of Office Act when he dismissed Edwin M. Stanton from his position as Secretary of War. Due to the alleged violation the House of Representatives voted eleven articles of impeachment against the President. In the spring of 1868, Andrew Johnson was acquitted of the charges against him by one vote.

The **Tenure of Office Act** was passed by the United States Congress on March 2, 1867. The act provided that all federal officials who are required to have Senate confirmation for their appointments could not be removed from office without the consent of the Senate. The entire act can be read by accessing http://teachingamericanhistory.org/library/index.asp?document=1922.

216

Maximilian and the French control of Mexico occurred in 1863 when French soldiers captured Mexico City. It was the hope of Napoleon III to set up a puppet government in Mexico. President Abraham Lincoln and the United States pledged support to Juarez and his government. In 1867, Juarez was finally able to vanquish Maximilian and Napoleon the III pulled his troops out of Mexico. Maximilian was executed by firing squad on June 19, 1867.

Benito Juarez took power in Mexico as her president in 1858 sparking the Reform War of 1858-1861. Abraham Lincoln was a strong supporter of Juarez and aided him by supplying arms and ammunition to the liberal cause. In addition, to General Sheridan came this order from General Grant, which of course originated with Lincoln: "Concentrate in all available points in the States an army strong enough to move against the invaders of Mexico."

Although the novel takes poetic license by insinuating that Juarez was determined to bring down the United States government in favor of the Confederacy, it is a fact that Juarez did just the opposite. He was approached by a delegation from the Confederate government led by John T. Pickett who wanted him to band with them in hopes of gaining Mexican support for the Confederacy. Juarez put Pickett in a Mexican jail for thirty days and then expelled him and his delegation from Mexico.

Import tariffs passed by Congress, beginning in 1828 with what Southerners called the Tariff of Abominations, were designed to help develop industry in the United States and also seemingly demonstrated favoritism toward the North, the industrial area of the country. The intent of passing the tariff was to force all states, but most especially the southern states, to purchase their needed imported goods from the North rather than the cheaper goods they could purchase from other nations, particularly England. The passing of the tariff resulted in the Nullification Crisis of the 1830s when South Carolina threatened secession due to the import tax. The tariff issue remained a problem right up until the Civil War began and is considered one of the factors that caused the war.

The **National Currency Bureau** was created on February 25, 1863 along with the position of Comptroller of Currency. The Bureau was necessitated by the newly passed act allowing Congress to print greenbacks. The notes were actually printed in secure locations outside of Washington DC and sent to the Bureau for finishing. In 1874 the Bureau, now called the **U.S. Bureau of Printing and Engraving,** was officially recognized. The author has taken poetic license in referring to the U.S. Bureau of Printing and Engraving over the lesser known name of National Currency Bureau.

A **pound of greenbacks**, or any U.S. currency is equal to 454 notes because the approximate weight of a currency notes is 1 gram and there are 454 grams in one pound.

A **pepper box** was a revolver created in the 1830s and so named because it resembled a household pepper grinder. It had three or more barrels grouped around a central axis and thus was a repeating or multi-shot firearm.

Bryson's Hotel in Liberty Hill, Texas was a stage coach stop run by John and Amelia Bryson. It began as a stop for the military stage coach line from Austin, Texas. The military coaches would stop at the spring on the Bryson property to water their horses. The military drivers convinced Bryson of the need for a public stage coach stop at Liberty Hill and the "hotel" was born.

The **Faubourg Marigny** was developed in the early 1800s by Bernard Xavier Philippe de Marigny de Mandeville, a Creole millionaire. The area was made up of land from his family plantation that was near the old city limits of New Orleans. The Faubourg Marigny was primarily designed for white Creole gentlemen to set up homes for their mistresses of color and their children. It was fashioned after the tradition of plaçage that recognized such assignations as common-law marriages. The Faubourg Marigny is adjacent to the French Quarter.

The **Bourbon Orleans Hotel** in New Orleans, Louisiana is the original site of the Orleans Ballroom built by John Davis in 1817 and the Orleans Theater which was built on land adjacent to the ballroom. Thus Davis established French Opera in the United States and later expanded the site as dining and gaming rooms that rivaled those in Europe.

Ursuline Academy of New Orleans was founded in 1727. It was noted for its exceptional education given to girls of wealthy city members as well as to female slaves, free women of color and Native Americans. The convent and the first school building were located on Chartres Street in the French Quarter.

Secretary of War, **Edwin Stanton**, held office from 1862 – 1868 when he was dismissed by President Andrew Johnson. While in office Stanton took over management of all telegraph lines in the country, he censored the press and kept full control over any news that reached the public.

Camp Douglas was located near Lake Michigan in Chicago. It was the northernmost prisoner of war camp during the Civil War and had the highest mortality rate of any Union civil war prison. It has been reported that one in five prisoners at Camp Douglas died within the prison walls.

Colonel Benjamin J. Sweet was commander of Camp Douglas from May 2, 1864 until all prisoners were released at the end of the Civil War.

Charity Hospital in New Orleans was founded in 1736 and is the second continuous public hospital in the United States. In the mid-1800s it was located on is what is now known as Basin Street.

Maria Laveau was one of several New Orleans Voodoo queens who plied their trade in the 1800s. She was a free person of color who was born in the late 1700s. She learned her craft from a voodoo doctor named Dr. John or John Bayou. Maria had fifteen children and numerous grandchildren.

Isaac T. Hinton was a publisher in New Orleans in the 1860s. His shop was located at 27 Commercial Place.

The **use of chloroform** during the Civil War, by doctors from both the South and North is attested to in field records and statistics and found in military archives.   .

The **Tremont House** in Galveston, Texas was built in 1839 and was frequented by Sam Houston, Ulysses S. Grant, Clara Barton, Edwin Booth and Buffalo Bill. It housed residents fleeing the 1900 storm and was graced by six United States presidents. The Tremont House still stands in Galveston but is located one-half block away from the original hotel.

Jean Lafitte was a privateer and smuggler who aided the United States during the War of 1812 at the Battle of New Orleans. Hoping to obtain a pardon from the U.S. government for his privateering because of the aid he gave to Andrew Jackson he petitioned Washington but the pardon was denied. So he moved his base of operation to Galveston in 1817. He called his colony on the island Campeche. When he was run off of the island he burned Campeche before he left.

The **Mier Expedition** was a border clash between Texans and Mexicans during the days of the Republic of Texas in 1842. **John C. Hill**, a boy of 13, went with his father and brothers to aid besieged San Antonio at the behest of a Texas Ranger from Jack Hays' company. The Hills joined with other Texans under General Alexander Somervell for a march to the Rio Grande and the Battle of Mier. John and many others were captured and marched to Mexico City. General Santa Ana ordered the death of the captives but revised the death sentence to every man who drew a black bean. The resultant 10%, or 17 men, were executed by firing squad. John C. Hill pleaded with Santa Ana for the release of his father and brother. Impressed by the boy's bravery, Santa Ana agreed to release them if John would remain in Mexico as his son.

The **cavern** that still exists in San Marcos, Texas and is now called Wonder World is a Texas State Historical Site and the only earthquake formed cave in the continental United States. The Balcones fault line is still an active fault line today.

Texas Wild Rice is found only in the Upper San Marcos River. Texas Wild Rice forms thick stands that host numerous aquatic invertebrates.

219

The plant can only pollinate neighboring plants that are within about 75 cm of the pollen-bearing plant.

The 10,000 foot **railroad trestle "causeway"** was built across Galveston Bay in 1860 providing train service from Galveston to Texas City and then on to Houston. During the Civil War Fort Hebert was built to help protect the railway. The Galveston-Houston railroad carried Confederate troops and munitions to Galveston Island via the causeway to break a Union blockade of Galveston Island in 1861.

The **Lakes of Killarney** are located in a mountain-ringed valley in County Kerry, Ireland. There are three lakes and they are a renowned tourist attraction.

An **Arkansas Toothpick** is the name used in Alabama, Tennessee and Georgia for knives similar to Bowie knives. They are heavy daggers with 12-20 inch blades. The knife is carefully weighted for throwing and is also used for slashing and thrusting.

George T. Ruby was an African American who held high positions in the Republican Party. He was the only African American delegate from Texas at the National Republican Convention of 1868. He was also elected as a delegate to the Texas' Constitutional Convention of 1868-69.

Norris W. Cuney was a leader in Galveston's local Republican Party and served in many positions of high office in his lifetime. In 1867 he aided the victims of the island's yellow fever epidemic.

E. M. Gregory was a Union Infantry commander and eventually an assistant commissioner of the Freedmen's Bureau for Texas and established a bureau headquarters at the customhouse in Galveston in 1865.

In 1867 the **local Galveston police force** was discharged due to clashes with citizens and white soldiers. It was replaced with a primarily African American force.

San Francisco de la Espada is one of five missions established by the Spanish in San Antonio in 1731. It is the southernmost of the five missions located on the San Antonio River. It was originally founded in east Texas as San Francisco de la Tejas.

The **Goodnight-Loving Trail** was blazed in 1866 as an alternative to market for cattle rounded up that had roamed free during the years of the Civil War. The trail was blazed by Charles Goodnight and Oliver Loving and covered from Texas through New Mexico, Colorado and into Wyoming. Fort Sumner, New Mexico was the first major stop for cattle selling along the trail.

Cherokee words used within the story:

A-i-sv E-lo-we-hi means Walks Silent

220

gv-ni-g-yo-na means black bear
E-Du-Da means great giver of all things
Tlanusi-yi means the Leech Place, the name the Cherokee gave to what is now Murphy, North Carolina
nu-na-hi-du-na-tlo-hi-lu-i means the trail where they cried

Existing places mentioned within the story:

The well known areas of:

Washington, DC is the capital of the United States of America. It was chosen as the site of the nation's capital in 1800 by George Washington. Pierre Charles L'Enfant was the designer of the city and the surveying and layout of the city was done by Benjamin Banneker, an African American mathematical genius. The streets mentioned in the novel all were part of the city in the 1860s.

Atlanta, Georgia is the capital city of the state of Georgia. It began as Fort Peachtree built in 1813 on the western edge of the American frontier in an area that was not at that time a part of the state of Georgia.

New Orleans, Louisiana was founded in 1718. Adrian de Pauger laid the city streets in 1721. The royal houses of France and Catholic saints are the namesakes of those streets. New Orleans remained part of colonial France until 1763 when it was sold to Spain. In 1803, New Orleans was sold to the United States by France as part of the Louisiana Purchase. France had reclaimed New Orleans and its former territories from Spain in 1800. All of the streets mentioned in New Orleans existed in the city during the 1860s.

Baltimore, Maryland was founded in 1729 and prospered as a commercial port. It later became the capital of the state of Maryland. During the War of 1812, Francis Scott Key wrote the national anthem of the United States while watching, from a ship in Baltimore Harbor, the attack of Fort McHenry by the British.

Indian Territory, part of which is now the state of Oklahoma was established in 1825 as all land lying west of the Mississippi River. It was later reduced to what is present day Oklahoma, Nebraska, Kansas, and part of Iowa.

Chattanooga, Tennessee was officially named in 1836. Prior to the naming it was called by two names: Ross's Landing and Lookout City. Ross's Landing was a trading post established by John Ross, chief of the Cherokee Indians, in 1816. The name Lookout City came from Lookout Mountain that begins in Chattanooga.

Houston, Texas was founded in 1836 by John Kirby Allen and Augustus Chapman Allen. The brothers envisioned the city as a commercial port with ships sailing up Buffalo Bayou from the Gulf of Mexico. Their dream became a reality, but not fully until 1914 when the Houston Ship Channel opened.

Galveston, Texas was designated a port of entry by Mexico in 1825 and a small customs house was established there in 1830 since Galveston was the best port between New Orleans and Veracruz. However the town was not officially founded until 1838 when Michel B. Menard and a group of investors received permission from the Republic of Texas to purchase 4,605 acres at the harbor in order to found a town. The Galveston streets used in the novel existed in the 1860s. **The Strand**, also known as Avenue B, parallels the bay. Since the city's inception it has been considered the heart of the business district and was known in the 1800s as the "Wall Street of the Southwest."

As a side note, Galveston is the boyhood home of the author.

San Antonio, Texas, the site of the Battle of the Alamo during the Texas Revolution from Mexico was first explored by Spanish expeditions in 1691 and again in 1709. The town of San Antonio grew out of San Antonio de Béxar Presidio which was founded in 1718. In 1773 San Antonio de Béxar became the capital of Spanish Texas.

Republic of Liberia: was founded in 1820 by free African-Americans and freed slaves from the United States. The country's name means land of the free. When Africans were found aboard slavers (ships that carried captured Africans to ports for sale) the Africans were often transported to Liberia and left there.

The following lesser known cities, towns, and areas also exist within the United States:

Blue Ridge, Georgia, the county seat of Fannin County, Georgia was founded by Colonel Mike McKinney in 1886 giving Fannin County a market for its agricultural products. Prior to 1886, the area was primarily called Fannin County. Fannin County was created in 1854 from portions of Union County and Gilmer County, with Morganton as the first county seat. The county is named for Colonel James Fannin who was a hero in the Texas War for Independence. The author used poetic license to include the town of Blue Ridge in the novel.

Ellijay, Georgia, the county seat of Gilmer County, was incorporated in 1834. In Cherokee it means "earth green there" and was the site of an Indian village. Cherokee lived in Ellijay until their removal from Georgia in 1838 to Indian Territory.

Mineral Bluff, Georgia is an unincorporated village north of Blue Ridge. It grew with the coming of the railroad to Blue Ridge and was known for its spa retreats and inspirational waters. Its heyday was in the late 1800s.

My Mountain is a mountain located between Mineral Bluff and Blue Ridge, Georgia

Murphy, North Carolina was named for the North Carolina politician, Archibald Murphey. Murphy originally started along the trading path known as the Unicoi Turnpike which connected the Cherokee lands east of the mountains with the "Overhill Towns" of Tennessee.

Robbinsville, North Carolina is part of 337 acres of land given to a prominent leader of the Cherokee, Junaluska. He and his warriors aided Andrew Jackson in a battle against the Creek Indians by swimming underwater to the bend of the Tallapoosa River and seizing the Creek canoes. In 1847 he walked from Indian Territory back to North Carolina. The North Carolina legislature then awarded Junaluska the land mentioned above, $100.00, and citizenship in North Carolina.

Copper Hill, Tennessee is one of two mining towns that served the Copper Basin of Tennessee. It was home to the Company of Copper Hill. The area was the largest metal producing mining operation in the Southeastern United States until 1987. The early owners of the mines gave no attention to the environment and were only interested in profiting from the land. They cut down trees and the metal operations produced acid rains that killed over 60,000 acres of land.

Ducktown, Tennessee was the site of the Burra Burra Mine. Ducktown was the other mining town servicing the Copper Basin. Ducktown and Copperhill were railroad towns that also made use of the Ocoee River Gorge to transport the loads of metal to the Tennessee River Valley.

Fightingtown Creek, Tennessee was the site of a Cherokee village that was established in 1835. More than 100 residents of the village were rounded up and sent along the Trail of Tears to Indian Territory in 1838.

The source of the **Hiawassee River** is on the north slope of Rocky Mountain in Towns County, Georgia. The river flows northward into North Carolina and eventually empties into the Tennessee River.

The **Nantahala River** is located in western North Carolina and its name comes from the Cherokee for "land of the noonday sun." The river flows into Fontana Lake after passing through a high narrow gorge. The sun often only reaches the river in the gorge during the middle of the day.

The **Valley River** flows southwest between Topton and Murphy, North Carolina for approximately 120 miles. It is a tributary of the Hiawassee River that begins in the Cherokee County Snowbird Mountains and descends 2,960 feet to enter the Hiawassee.

Liberty Hill, Texas lies thirty-three miles northwest of Austin between the north and south forks of the San Gabriel River. In 1853 William Oliver Spencer, the postmaster, suggested its name.

Author's Note

For some people, writing a book may be a one person affair, but for my novels an entire family is required, which is why I need to acknowledge the contributions of my wife and my two daughters. My wife, Chris did an enormous amount of editing and contributed ideas to the book. My daughter, Kara, did a great deal of research for it. And the cover idea came from my daughter, Christi. My 92-year-old mother also offered her help in editing, especially regarding proper English grammar.

So if you have any criticisms contact the four people mentioned above and leave me out of it.

In addition to my immediate family, I would also like to acknowledge my cousin, Tipton Golias and his wife, Ann for the ideas they contributed, their editing efforts and the publishing of this novel.

I once again shamelessly borrowed heavily from actual people in the creation of my characters. I mentioned that fact in the Acknowledgement of my first novel *When the Night Bird Called, the Saga of Caleb Quinn.*

At this time I would like to further recognize the "models" that were responsible for many of the characters from the first novel and those who served as a basis for some of the new characters introduced in this novel.

Beau Carroll is a childhood friend of the author's daughter, Kara and a well-known figure in Beaumont, Texas real estate circles.
Phillip Buckner, AKA Ronald Phillips is a surrogate son of the Coryells and now lives in Houston, Texas…he is as strong and intelligent as depicted by his character.
Lucinda Baker was patterned after the author's aunt and Tipton's mother, a very kind and tough-minded lady.
Captain (Whitey) Varvil, a lifelong seaman, who retired from the Galveston-Bolivar ferry system as a commodore, was married to the author's aunt after whom Lucinda's character was developed.
Matthew and Samantha Moore are actually Matt and Sam Mealer, neighbors and good friends of the author when he lived in Mineral Bluff, Georgia. They are strong, intelligent, warm people who were accurately depicted in the novels.
Eryn and Emmilou (AKA Emily Savannah) are the Mealer's two daughters.

Tip Thomas is patterned after Tipton Golias. Tipton is the author's cousin and friend since infancy.

Ann Thomas, the wife of Tip Thomas is actually the wife of Tipton Golias.

Gram Szelgia, named for the paternal grandmother of the author's wife was actually modeled after the author's maternal grandmother.

Rags Webber is patterned after a good friend of the author, Reggie Webber, the service manager of Helena Laboratories. He resides in Beaumont, Texas.

Shannon Edwards is actually the author's niece, Shannon Pokusa. She has pestered the author since her early childhood with her incessant talking.

Doc Randolph is the older brother of one of the author's former little league players, Josh. Mark Randolph now practices medicine near Austin, Texas.

Jasper Lovoi is a childhood friend of the author's son, Don. The Lovoi family and the Coryell family have been friends for 30 years. Jasper currently resides in Houston.

John Finley is head of the printing department at Helena Laboratories. He is a good friend of the author and has a vast knowledge of the history of U.S. currency.

Chris Coleman, known in the novel simply as Mister Coleman, coached the author's son in basketball at West Brook High School in Beaumont, Texas. He now resides in Jasper, Texas.

Tony Torres was a childhood friend of the author. Like the author he spent much of his summers at the Galveston YMCA. Tony retired from the navy.

Richi Torres, Tony's younger brother, is now retired and living in Round Rock, Texas. After not seeing each other for 50 years he was cruel enough to defeat the author in a game of golf.

Ricco, Jesse, and Rudy were neighborhood pals of the author who grew up with him in Galveston.

The McNulty family, James, Mary Elizabeth, Kerry (Kerri) and Danielle are actually the Pokusa family and the parents and sisters of Shannon Pokusa. James is the brother-in-law of the author.

Joe Pokusa was the author's father-in-law and a man devoted to his family.

Resources

http://digital.library.okstate.edu/encyclopedia/entries/i/in018.html
http://donchesnut.com/genealogy/pages/cherokee.htm
http://ellijay.georgia.gov/05/home/0,2230,9008395,00.html;jsessionid=C737C5663D7B46
5EB504B60121E1F365
http://en.wikipedia.org/wiki/Faubourg_Marigny
http://en.wikipedia.org/wiki/Hiwassee_River
http://en.wikipedia.org/wiki/Ku_Klux_Klan
http://en.wikipedia.org/wiki/Maximilian_I_of_Mexico
http://en.wikipedia.org/wiki/Nantahala_River
http://en.wikipedia.org/wiki/Valley_River
http://gatewayno.com/history/Lafitte.html
http://goneworleans.about.com/od/tours/a/historyofno.htm
http://ilovemurphy.com/2009/01/28/overview-of-murphy-north-carolina-the-location-
population-people-real-estate-history-and-facts/
http://law2.umkc.edu/faculty/projects/ftrials/impeach/imp_tenure.html
http://moneyfactory.gov/historytimeline.html
http://nucleus.bio.txstate.edu/~pfw/docs/Edwards%20Aquifer%20&%20San%20Marcos%
20River%20Field%20Guide.pdf
http://roadsidegeorgia.com/city/atlanta01.html
http://theblueridgehighlander.com/history/north_georgia_mountains/fannin-county.php
http://theblueridgehighlander.com/polk_county_tennessee/index.php
http://washington.org/visiting/experience-dc/knowledge-seeker/dc-history-african-
american
http://whitehouse.gov1.info/visit/tour.html
http://www.9key.com/markers/marker_detail.asp?atlas_number=5167012625
http://www.blueridgemountains.com/history.html
http://www.bourbonorleans.com/french-quarter-hotel-history.php
http://www.brainyquote.com/quotes/authors/t/thomas_jefferson.html#ixzz1GQP3RG1D
http://www.censusdiggins.com/prison_camp_douglas.html
http://www.chattanoogafun.com/history/
http://www.cherokee-nc.com/index.php?page=62
http://www.civilwarmedicalbooks.com/chloroform_Civil_War.html
http://www.csicop.org/sb/show/secrets_of_the_voodoo_tomb/
http://www.exchangerate.com/us_currency_fun_facts.html
http://www.galveston.com/thetremonthouse/history.html
http://www.hellobaltimore.com/history.cfm
http://www.lsjunction.com/facts/missions.htm
http://www.mclno.org/MCLNO/Menu/Hospital/History/CharitysBeginnings.aspx
http://www.mexconnect.com/articles/274-mexico-s-lincoln-the-ecstasy-and-agony-of-
benito-juarez
http://www.nationaltota.org/general-info/
http://www.nationaltota.org/the-story/
http://www.ocoeeinfo.com/history.html
http://www.pbs.org/weta/thewest/people/d_h/goodnight.htm
http://www.pbs.org/wgbh/aia/part4/4h1567.html
http://www.pbs.org/wnet/jimcrow/stories_org_kkk.html
http://www.spartacus.schoolnet.co.uk/USASstanton.htm
http://www.state.gov/r/pa/ei/bgn/6618.htm
http://thestrand.com/history/beginnings.php
http://www.tshaonline.org/handbook/online
http://www.tsl.state.tx.us/exhibits/forever/freedom/page7.html
http://www.whitehouse.gov/about/presidents/andrewjohnson
http://www.wisconsinhistory.org/dictionary/index.asp?action=view&term_id=2403&searc
h=term=doolittle